RAINBOW CLASSICS

General Editor: May Lamberton Becker

Denis Christopher Meredith

July 1946

J. WALKER McSPADDEN

robin hood and

His Merry Outlaws

Illustrated by Louis Slobodkin

With an Introduction written by

May Lamberton Becker

THE WORLD PUBLISHING COMPANY

CLEVELAND AND NEW YORK

Rainbow Classics ARE PUBLISHED BY
The World Publishing Company, 2231 West 110th Street, Cleveland 2, Ohio

FIRST PRINTING APRIL 1946

Contents

INTRODUCTION

how this book came to be written

BY MAY LAMBERTON BECKER

ONCE upon a time—a long time ago, for the first book about him was printed in 1520 and his was an old story then—a brave, gallant gentleman who had run through his fortune and couldn't pay his bills was outlawed for debt and took to the woods of Northern England. They were deep woods, full of the King's deer and all sorts of game; Sherwood Forest then was twenty miles long and eight broad, spreading over a hundred thousand acres, and an outlaw could live there well enough if the sheriff did not catch him. If he had good friends with him, he could live very happily. So, as this gallant gentleman was far too quick for the Sheriff of Nottingham, and as the friends he gathered round him were as brave and as merry as he, this Robyn Hode, as his name was spelled in those days, held what amounted to a court of his own and lived in the greenwood a life everyone since has envied.

For his friends were all chosen because they were fine fellows. When he heard of someone especially skilful and courageous, he would go in disguise to try him in all sorts of ways, and if he seemed the right sort, would invite him to join the band. Thus "Little" John Nailor, the giant, became one of them; and William Scadlock, whom we know as Will Scarlet; Much, the miller's son; George-a-Green, the poundkeeper; a jolly friar whose name was Tuck; the romantic Allan-a-Dale; and later on a young lady known as Maid Marian, who may have been Matilda, daughter of Lord Fitzwalter. In time there were one hundred archers in Robin Hood's band, but not one of them, good as he was at archery, could beat Robin himself at the long bow, and no one ever has done so. Their clothes were green, so that you could scarcely see them among the green leaves.

When rich men travelled through the dark forest they went strongly guarded, for Robin Hood's men were robbers. Nobody ever loved robbers so well as these were loved by the common people and the poor. They killed no man unless he attacked them, and no woman was ever hurt. Most humane of robbers, they fed the poor with what they took from the rich; it was a sort of wild justice making up for the way in which wealthy and powerful people then oppressed the poor. Robin disliked the clergy because they were so rich, but he was a good Christian; his tombstone stood for many years beside the roadway, saying

> . . . Never archer as he so good
> And people called him Robin Hood.
> Such outlaws as he and his men
> Will England never see again.

A festival in Robin Hood's memory was held every year for centuries. It was the great day of the people and the poor, and whenever the law tried to stop it—for its merry-making was boisterous—the people rebelled and rioted. Plays and dances from these festivals kept his memory green long after the festivals were no longer celebrated. Then, too, the adventures of his merry men were told in song and in countless little books sold to country people at fairs and were always very popular with children. One reason why legends of Robin Hood have come down to us so little changed is that long before they were printed they were sung as ballads, whose tunes were easy to pick up and whose rhymes were hard to forget. These ballads go back to the thirteenth century—the famous *Vision of Piers Plowman,* written in the fourteenth century, speaks of "Robin the ribald with his rusty language" as if everybody knew who he was, as indeed everybody did. Verses from some of these ancient ballads are woven into the stories in this book: you are to imagine one voice singing the verse and the whole company coming in on the refrain "With a hey down down a down down." As some of the ballads had a vast number of stanzas—one had one hundred and ninety-three—this sort of singing could keep everyone happy for a long while, and in time everyone would pick up the words.

Robin's real name seems to have been Robert Fitzooth. He was born about 1160. Some think he was a Norman noble, the rightful Earl of Huntingdon; others that he was a Saxon yeoman. Whoever he may have been in the beginning, he was real and alive, and he and his companions have gone right on living unto this day. There is something about their way of life that charms everyone, old or young. No wonder this book is a children's classic; all sorts of children have made it so. A boy once wrote me that before he was twelve his favorite story had been

"Robin Hood"; he and his friends used to act it out, day after day. That was all he said about himself, but he had written, in a careful hand, on the letter-paper of a school for the blind.

So I am not one of those who say there never was a "real" Robin Hood. I agree with a famous judge in England, Edward Abbott Parry, who wrote about him: "My mind remains young enough, I am glad to say, to believe in the great truths I learned in the nursery."

Adventures such as these suit the adventurous spirit of Louis Slobodkin, who made for them these robust, exciting pictures. His grandfather was a cowboy in the Ukraine, his father an inventor in Albany. When he was ten he made his first piece of sculpture—Benjamin Franklin in modelling wax, complete with spectacles. It was as an architectural sculptor that his fame began; his heroic bronze of Lincoln is in the Department of the Interior at Washington. Meanwhile he had shipped as deckhand to the Argentine on a freighter and found inspiration for his work among the sailors; his statue of the ship's carpenter with his concertina was sent around this country and then to England with the Good-Will Tour of American Sculpture. In 1941 he made a brilliant entry into illustration of children's books and three years later won the Caldecott Medal for his illustration of James Thurber's *Many Moons*. The life of the beloved outlaw Robin Hood has given Slobodkin an outlet for his own bounding vitality and love of fun, while his warm interest in the period brings back for us the flavor and character of the time in which that daring outlaw lived.

robin hood and His Merry Outlaws

I

how Robin Hood Became an Outlaw

List and hearken, gentlemen,
  That be of free-born blood,
I shall you tell of a good yeoman
  His name was Robin Hood.
Robin was a proud outlaw,
  While as he walked on the ground:
So courteous an outlaw as he was one
  Was never none else found.

In the days of good King Harry the Second of England—he of the warring sons—there were certain forests in the north country set aside for the King's hunting, and no man might shoot deer therein under penalty of death. These forests were guarded by the King's Foresters, the chief of whom, in each wood, was no mean man but equal in authority to the Sheriff in his walled town, or even to my lord Bishop in his abbey.

One of the greatest of royal preserves was Sherwood and Barnesdale forests near the two towns of Nottingham and Barnesdale. Here for some years dwelt one, Hugh Fitzooth as Head Forester, with his good wife and little son Robert. The boy had been born in Lockesley town—

13

in the year 1160, stern records say,—and was often called
Lockesley, or Rob of Lockesley.   He was a comely, well-
knit stripling, and as soon as he was strong enough to walk
his chief delight was to go with his father into the forest.
As soon as his right arm received thew and sinew he
learned to draw the long bow and speed a true arrow.
While on winter evenings his greatest joy was to hear his
father tell of bold Will o' the Green, the outlaw, who for
many summers defied the King's Foresters and feasted
with his men upon King's deer.   And on other stormy days
the boy learned to whittle out a straight shaft for the long
bow, and tip it with gray goose feathers.

The fond mother sighed when she saw the boy's face
light up at these woodland tales.   She was of gentle birth,
and had hoped to see her son famous at court or abbey.
She taught him to read and write, to doff his cap without
awkwardness and to answer directly and truthfully both
lord and peasant.   But the boy, although he took kindly to
these lessons of breeding, was yet happiest when he had
his beloved bow in hand and strolled at will, listening to
the murmur of the trees.

Two playmates had Rob in these gladsome early days.
One was Will Gamewell, his father's brother's son, who
lived at Gamewell Lodge, hard by Nottingham town.
The other was Marian Fitzwalter, only child of the Earl
of Huntingdon.   The castle of Huntingdon could be seen
from the top of one of the tall trees in Sherwood; and on
more than one bright day Rob's white signal from his tree
told Marian that he awaited her there: for you must know
that Rob did not visit her at the castle.   His father and her
father were enemies.   Some people whispered that Hugh
Fitzooth was the rightful Earl of Huntingdon, but that he

had been defrauded out of his lands by Fitzwalter, who had won the King's favor by a crusade to the Holy Land. But little cared Rob or Marian for this enmity, however it had arisen. They knew that the great greenwood was open to them, and that the wide, wide world was full of the scent of flowers and the song of birds.

Days of youth speed all too swiftly, and troubled skies come all too soon. Rob's father had two other enemies besides Fitzwalter in the persons of the lean Sheriff of Nottingham and the fat Bishop of Hereford. These three enemies one day got possession of the King's ear and whispered therein to such good—or evil—purpose that Hugh Fitzooth was removed from his post of King's Forester. He and his wife and Rob, then a youth of nineteen, were descended upon, during a cold winter's evening, and dispossessed without warning. The Sheriff arrested the Forester for treason,—of which, poor man, he was as guiltless as you or I,—and carried him to Nottingham jail. Rob and his mother were sheltered over night in the jail, also, but next morning were roughly bade to go about their business. Thereupon they turned for succor to their only kinsman, Squire George of Gamewell, who sheltered them in all kindness.

But the shock, and the winter night's journey, proved too much for Dame Fitzooth. She had not been strong for some time before leaving the forest. In less than two months she was no more. Rob felt as though his heart was broken at this loss. But scarcely had the first spring flowers begun to blossom upon her grave, when he met another crushing blow in the loss of his father. That stern man had died in prison before his accusers could agree upon the charges by which he was to be brought to trial.

Two years passed by. Rob's cousin Will was away at school; and Marian's father, who had learned of her friendship with Rob, had sent his daughter to the court of Queen Eleanor. So these years were lonely ones to the orphaned lad. The bluff old Squire was kind to him, but secretly could make nothing of one who went about brooding and as though seeking for something he had lost. The truth is that Rob missed his old life in the forest no less than his mother's gentleness, and his father's companionship. Every time he twanged the string of the long bow against his shoulder and heard the gray goose shaft sing, it told him of happy days that he could not recall.

One morning as Rob came in to breakfast, his uncle greeted him with, "I have news for you, Rob, my lad!" and the hearty old Squire finished his draught of ale and set his pewter tankard down with a crash.

"What may that be, Uncle Gamewell?" asked the young man.

"Here is a chance to exercise your good long bow and win a pretty prize. The Fair is on at Nottingham, and the Sheriff proclaims an archer's tournament. The best fellows are to have places with the King's Foresters, and the one who shoots straightest of all will win for prize a golden arrow—a useless bauble enough, but just the thing for your lady love, eh, Rob my boy?" Here the Squire laughed and whacked the table again with his tankard.

Rob's eyes sparkled. "'Twere indeed worth shooting for, uncle mine," he said. "I should dearly love to let arrow fly alongside another man. And a place among the Foresters is what I have long desired. Will you let me try?"

"To be sure," rejoined his uncle. "Well I know that

your good mother would have had me make a clerk of you;
but well I see that the greenwood is where you will pass
your days. So, here's luck to you in the bout!" And the
huge tankard came a third time into play.

The young man thanked his uncle for his good wishes,
and set about making preparations for the journey. He
traveled lightly; but his yew bow must needs have a new
string, and his clothyard arrows must be of the straightest
and soundest.

One fine morning, a few days after, Rob might have been
seen passing by way of Lockesley through Sherwood
Forest to Nottingham town. Briskly walked he and gaily,
for his hopes were high and never an enemy had he in the
wide world. But 'twas the very last morning in all his life
when he was to lack an enemy! For, as he went his way
through Sherwood, whistling a blithe tune, he came suddenly upon a group of Foresters, making merry beneath
the spreading branches of an oak-tree. They had a huge
meat pie before them and were washing down prodigious
slices of it with nut brown ale.

One glance at the leader and Rob knew at once that he
had found an enemy. 'Twas the man who had usurped
his father's place as Head Forester, and who had roughly
turned his mother out in the snow. But never a word said
he for good or bad, and would have passed on his way, had
not this man, clearing his throat with a huge gulp, bellowed out: "By my troth here is a pretty little archer!
Where go you, my lad, with that tupenny bow and toy
arrows? Belike he would shoot at Nottingham Fair! Ho!
Ho!"

A roar of laughter greeted this sally. Rob flushed, for
he was mightily proud of his shooting.

"My bow is as good as yours," he retorted, "and my shafts will carry as straight and as far. So I'll not take lessons of any of ye!"

They laughed again loudly at this, and the leader said with a frown:

"Show us some of your skill, and if you can hit the mark here's twenty silver pennies for you. But if you hit it not you are in for a sound drubbing for your pertness."

"Pick your own target," quoth Rob in a fine rage. "I'll lay my head against that purse that I can hit it."

"It shall be as you say," retorted the Forester angrily, "your head for your sauciness that you hit not my target."

Now at a little rise in the wood a herd of deer came grazing by, distant full fivescore yards. They were King's deer but at that distance seemed safe from any harm. The Head Forester pointed to them.

"If your young arm could speed a shaft for half that distance, I'd shoot with you."

"Done!" cried Rob. "My head against twenty pennies I'll cause yon fine fellow in the lead of them to breathe his last."

And without more ado he tried the string of his long bow, placed a shaft thereon, and drew it to his ear. A moment, and the quivering string sang death as the shaft whistled across the glade. Another moment and the leader of the herd leaped high in his tracks and fell prone, dyeing the sward with his heart's blood.

A murmur of amazement swept through the Foresters and then a growl of rage. He that had wagered was angriest of all.

"Know you what you have done, rash youth?" he said. "You have killed a King's deer, and by the laws of King Harry your head remains forfeit. Talk not to me of pennies but get ye gone straight, and let me not look upon your face again."

Rob's blood boiled within him, and he uttered a rash speech. "I have looked upon your face once too often already, my fine Forester. 'Tis you who wear my father's shoes."

And with this he turned upon his heel and strode away.

The Forester heard his parting thrust with an oath. Red with rage he seized his bow, strung an arrow, and without warning launched it full at Rob. Well was it for the latter that the Forester's foot turned on a twig at the critical instant, for as it was the arrow whizzed by his ear so close as to take a stray strand of his hair with it.

Rob turned upon his assailant, now twoscore yards away.

"Ha!" said he. "You shoot not so straight as I for all your bravado. Take this from the tupenny bow!"

Straight flew his answering shaft. The Head Forester gave one cry then fell face downward and lay still. His life had avenged Rob's father, but the son was outlawed. Forward he ran through the forest, before the band could gather their scattered wits—still forward into the great greenwood. The swaying trees seemed to open their arms to the wanderer, and to welcome him home.

Toward the close of that same day, Rob paused hungry and weary at the cottage of a poor widow who dwelt upon the outskirts of the forest. Now this widow had often greeted him kindly in his boyhood days, giving him to eat and drink. So he boldly entered her door. The old dame was right glad to see him, and baked him cakes in the ashes, and had him rest and tell her his story. Then she shook her head.

" 'Tis an evil wind that blows through Sherwood," she

said. "The poor are despoiled and the rich ride over their
bodies. My three sons have been outlawed for shooting
King's deer to keep us from starving, and now hide in the
wood. An they tell me that twoscore of as good men as
ever drew bow are in hiding with them."

"Where are they, good mother?" cried Rob. "By my
faith, I will join them."

"Nay, nay," replied the old woman at first. But when
she saw that there was no other way, she said: "My sons
will visit me to-night. Stay you here and see them if you
must."

So Rob stayed willingly to see the widow's sons that
night, for they were men after his own heart. And when
they found that his mood was with them, they made him
swear an oath of fealty, and told him the haunt of the band
—a place he knew right well. Finally one of them said:

"But the band lacks a leader,—one who can use his head
as well as his hand. So we have agreed that he who has
skill enough to go to Nottingham, an outlaw, and win the
prize at archery, shall be our chief."

Rob sprang to his feet. "Said in good time!" cried he,
"for I had started to that self-same Fair, and all the Foresters, and all the Sheriff's men in Christendom shall not
stand between me and the centre of their target!"

And though he was but barely grown he stood so
straight and his eye flashed with such fire that the three
brothers seized his hand and shouted:

"A Lockesley! a Lockesley! if you win the golden arrow
you shall be chief of outlaws in Sherwood Forest!"

So Rob fell to planning how he could disguise himself
to go to Nottingham town; for he knew that the Foresters
had even then set a price on his head in the market-place.

It was even as Rob had surmised. The Sheriff of Nottingham posted a reward of two hundred pounds for the capture, dead or alive, of one Robert Fitzooth, outlaw. And the crowds thronging the streets upon that busy Fair day often paused to read the notice and talk together about the death of the Head Forester.

But what with wrestling bouts, and fights with quarterstaves, and songs by wandering minstrels, there came up so many other things to talk about, that the reward was forgotten for the nonce, and only the Foresters and Sheriff's men watched the gates with diligence, the Sheriff indeed spurring them to effort by offers of largess. His hatred of the father had descended to the son.

The great event of the day came in the afternoon. It was the archer's contest for the golden arrow, and twenty men stepped forth to shoot. Among them was a beggarman, a sorry looking fellow with leggings of different colors, and brown scratched face and hands. Over a tawny shock of hair he had a hood drawn much like that of a monk. Slowly he limped to his place in the line while the mob shouted in derision. But the contest was open to all comers, so no man said him nay.

Side by side with Rob—for it was he—stood a muscular fellow of swarthy visage and with one eye hid by a green bandage. Him also the crowd jeered, but he passed them by with indifference while he tried his bow with practiced hand.

A great crowd had assembled in the amphitheatre enclosing the lists. All the gentry and populace of the surrounding country were gathered there in eager expectancy. The central box contained the lean, but pompous Sheriff, his bejeweled wife, and their daughter, a supercilious young woman enough, who, it was openly hinted, was hoping to receive the golden arrow from the victor and thus be crowned queen of the day.

Next to the Sheriff's box was one occupied by the fat Bishop of Hereford; while on the other side was a box wherein sat a girl whose dark hair, dark eyes, and fair features caused Rob's heart to leap. 'Twas Maid Marian! She had come up for a visit from the Queen's court at London town and now sat demurely by her father, the Earl of Huntingdon. If Rob had been grimly resolved to win the arrow before, the sight of her sweet face multiplied his determination an hundredfold. He felt his muscles tightening into bands of steel, tense and true. Yet withal his heart would throb, making him quake in a most unaccountable way.

Then the trumpet sounded, and the crowd became silent while the herald announced the terms of the contest. The lists were open to all comers. The first target was to be placed at thirty ells distance, and all those who hit its centre were allowed to shoot at the second target, placed ten ells farther off. The third target was to be removed yet farther until the winner was proved. The winner was to receive the golden arrow and a place with the King's Foresters. He it was also who crowned the queen of the day.

The trumpet sounded again, and the archers prepared to shoot. Rob looked to his string, while the crowd smiled and whispered at the odd figure he cut with his vari-colored legs and little cape. But as the first man shot, they grew silent.

The target was not so far but that twelve out of the twenty contestants reached its inner circle. Rob shot sixth in the line and landed fairly, being rewarded by an

approving grunt from the man with the green blinder,
who shot seventh, and with apparent carelessness, yet
true to the bulls-eye.

The mob cheered and yelled themselves hoarse at this
even marksmanship. The trumpet sounded again, and a
new target was set up at forty ells.

The first three archers again struck true, amid the loud
applause of the onlookers; for they were general favorites
and expected to win. Indeed 'twas whispered that each
was backed by one of the three dignitaries of the day.
The fourth and fifth archers barely grazed the centre.
Rob fitted his arrow quietly and with some confidence
sped it unerringly toward the shining circle.

"The beggar! the beggar!" yelled the crowd; "another
bull for the beggar!"

In truth his shaft was nearer the centre than any of the
others. But it was not so near that "Blinder," as the mob
had promptly christened his neighbor, did not place his
shaft just within the mark. Again the crowd cheered
wildly. Such shooting as this was not seen every day in
Nottingham town.

The other archers in this round were disconcerted by
the preceding shots, or unable to keep the pace. They
missed one after another and dropped moodily back, while
the trumpet sounded for the third round, and the target
was set up fifty ells distant.

"By my halidom you draw a good bow, young master,"
said Rob's queer comrade to him in the interval allowed
for rest. "Do you wish me to shoot first on this trial?"

"Nay," said Rob, "but you are a good fellow by this
token, and if I win not, I hope you may keep the prize
from yon strutters." And he nodded scornfully at the
three other archers who were surrounded by their ad-

mirers, and were being made much of by retainers of the
Sheriff, the Bishop, and the Earl. From them his eye
wandered toward Maid Marian's booth. She had been
watching him, it seemed, for their eyes met; then hers
were hastily averted.

"Blinder's" quick eye followed those of Rob. "A fair
maid, that," he said smilingly, "and one more worthy the
golden arrow than the Sheriff's haughty miss."

Rob looked at him swiftly and saw naught but kindli-
ness in his glance.

"You are a shrewd fellow and I like you well," was his
only comment.

Now the archers prepared to shoot again, each with
some little care. The target seemed hardly larger than the
inner ring had looked, at the first trial. The first three
sped their shafts, and while they were fair shots they did
not more than graze the inner circle.

Rob took his stand with some misgiving. Some fleck-
ing clouds overhead made the light uncertain, and a hand-
ful of wind frolicked across the range in a way quite disturbing to a bow-man's nerves. His eyes wandered for a
brief moment to the box wherein sat the dark-eyed girl.
His heart leaped! she met his glance and smiled at him
reassuringly. And in that moment he felt that she knew
him despite his disguise and looked to him to keep the
honor of old Sherwood. He drew his bow firmly and,
taking advantage of a momentary lull in the breeze,
launched the arrow straight and true—singing across the
range to the centre of the target.

"The beggar! the beggar! a bull! a bull!" yelled the fickle
mob, who from jeering him were now his warm friends.
"Can you beat that, Blinder?"

The last archer smiled scornfully and made ready. He

Straight flew his answering shaft. (Page 19)

drew his bow with ease and grace and, without seeming to study the course, released the winged arrow. Forward it leaped toward the target, and all eyes followed its flight. A loud uproar broke forth when it alighted, just without the centre and grazing the shaft sent by Rob. The stranger made a gesture of surprise when his own eyes announced the result to him, but saw his error. He had not allowed for a fickle gust of wind which seized the arrow and carried it to one side. But for all that he was the first to congratulate the victor.

"I hope we may shoot again," quoth he. "In truth I care not for the golden bauble and wished to win it in despite of the Sheriff for whom I have no love. Now crown the lady of your choice." And turning suddenly he was lost in the crowd, before Rob could utter what it was upon his lips to say, that he would shoot again with him.

And now the herald summoned Rob to the Sheriff's box to receive the prize.

"You are a curious fellow enough," said the Sheriff, biting his lip coldly; "yet you shoot well. What name go you by?"

Marian sat near and was listening intently.

"I am called Rob the Stroller, my Lord Sheriff," said the archer.

Marian leaned back and smiled.

"Well, Rob the Stroller, with a little attention to your skin and clothes you would not be so bad a man," said the Sheriff. "How like you the idea of entering my service?"

"Rob the Stroller has ever been a free man, my Lord, and desires no service."

The Sheriff's brow darkened, yet for the sake of his daughter and the golden arrow he dissembled.

"Rob the Stroller," said he, "here is the golden arrow

which has been offered to the best of archers this day.
You are awarded the prize. See that you bestow it
worthily."

At this point the herald nudged Rob and half inclined
his head toward the Sheriff's daughter, who sat with a thin
smile upon her lips. But Rob heeded him not. He took
the arrow and strode to the next box where sat Maid
Marian.

"Lady," he said, "pray accept this little pledge from a
poor stroller who would devote the best shafts in his
quiver to serve you."

"My thanks to you, Rob in the Hood," replied she with
a roguish twinkle in her eye; and she placed the gleaming
arrow in her hair, while the people shouted, "The Queen!
the Queen!"

The Sheriff glowered furiously upon this ragged archer
who had refused his service, taken his prize without a
word of thanks, and snubbed his daughter. He would
have spoken, but his proud daughter restrained him. He
called to his guard and bade them watch the beggar.
But Rob had already turned swiftly, lost himself in the
throng, and headed straight for the town gate.

That same evening within a forest glade a group of men
—some twoscore clad in Lincoln green—sat round a fire
roasting venison and making merry. Suddenly a twig
crackled and they sprang to their feet and seized their
weapons.

"I look for the widow's sons," a clear voice said, "and I
come alone."

Instantly the three men stepped forward.

" 'Tis Rob!" they cried; "welcome to Sherwood Forest,
Rob!" And all the men came and greeted him; for they
had heard his story.

Then one of the widow's sons, Stout Will, stepped forth and said:

"Comrades all, ye know that our band has sadly lacked a leader—one of birth, breeding, and skill. Belike we have found that leader in this young man. And I and my brothers have told him that the band would choose that one who should bring the Sheriff to shame this day and capture his golden arrow. Is it not so?"

The band gave assent.

Will turned to Rob. "What news bring you from Nottingham town?" asked he.

Rob laughed. "In truth I brought the Sheriff to shame for mine own pleasure and won his golden arrow to boot. But as to the prize ye must e'en take my word, for I bestowed it upon a maid."

And seeing the men stood in doubt at this, he continued: "But I'll gladly join your band, an you take me, as a common archer. For there are others older and mayhap more skilled than I."

Then stepped one forward from the rest, a tall swarthy man. And Rob recognized him as the man with the green blinder; only this was now removed, and his freed eye gleamed as stoutly as the other one.

"Rob in the Hood—for such the lady called you,"—said he, "I can vouch for your tale. You shamed the Sheriff e'en as I had hoped to do; and we can forego the golden arrow since it is in such fair hands. As to your shooting and mine, we must let future days decide. But here I, Will Stutely, declare that I will serve none other chief save only you."

Then good Will Stutely told the outlaws of Rob's deeds, and gave him his hand of fealty. And the widow's sons did likewise and the other members, every one, right gladly; because Will Stutely had heretofore been the truest bow in all the company. And they toasted him in nut brown ale, and hailed him as their leader, by the name of Robin Hood. And he accepted that name because Maid Marian had said it.

By the light of the camp-fire the band exchanged signs and passwords. They gave Robin Hood a horn upon which he was to blow to summon them. They swore, also, that while they might take money and goods from the unjust rich, they would aid and befriend the poor and the helpless; and that they would harm no woman, be she maid, wife, or widow. They swore all this with solemn oaths, while they feasted about the ruddy blaze, under the greenwood tree.

And that is how Robin Hood became an outlaw.

II

how Robin Hood Met Little John

"O here is my hand," the stranger
  reply'd,
  "I'll serve you with all my whole
  heart:
My name is John Little, a man of good
  mettle;
  Ne'er doubt me for I'll play my part."
"His name shall be altered," quoth
  William Stutely,
  "And I will his godfather be:
Prepare then a feast, and none of the
  least,
  For we will be merry," quoth he.

ALL that summer Robin Hood and
his merry men roamed in Sherwood Forest, and the fame
of their deeds ran abroad in the land. The Sheriff of Nottingham waxed wroth at the report but all his traps and
excursions failed to catch the outlaws. The poor people
began by fearing them, but when they found that the men
in Lincoln green who answered Robin Hood's horn meant
them no harm, but bespoiled the oppressor to relieve the
oppressed, they 'gan to have great liking for them. And
the band increased by other stout hearts till by the end of

29

the summer fourscore good men and true had sworn
fealty.

But the days of quiet which came on grew irksome to
Robin's adventurous spirit. Up rose he one gay morn,
and slung his quiver over his shoulders.

"This fresh breeze stirs the blood, my lads," quoth he,
"and I would be seeing what the gay world looks like in
the direction of Nottingham town. But tarry ye behind
in the borders of the forest, within earshot of my bugle
call."

Thus saying he strode merrily forward to the edge of
the wood, and paused there a moment, his agile form
erect, his brown locks flowing and his brown eyes watching the road; and a goodly sight he made, as the wind
blew the ruddy color into his cheeks.

The highway led clear in the direction of the town and
thither he boldly directed his steps. But at a bend in the
road he knew of a by-path leading across a brook which
made the way nearer and less open, into which he turned.
As he approached the stream he saw that it had become
swollen by recent rains into quite a pretty torrent. The
log foot-bridge was still there, but at this end of it a puddle
intervened which could be crossed only with a leap, if you
would not get your feet wet. But Robin cared little for
such a handicap. Taking a running start, his nimble legs
carried him easily over and balanced neatly upon the end
of the broad log. But he was no sooner started across than
he saw a tall stranger coming from the other side. Thereupon Robin quickened his pace, and the stranger did likewise, each thinking to cross first. Midway they met, and
neither would yield an inch.

"Give way, fellow!" roared Robin, whose leadership of
a band, I am afraid, had not tended to mend his manners.

The stranger smiled.   He was almost a head taller than the other.

"Nay," he retorted, "fair and softly!   I give way only to a better man than myself."

"Give way, I say," repeated Robin, "or I shall have to show you a better man."

His opponent budged not an inch but laughed loudly. "Now by my halidom!" he said good-naturedly, "I would not move after hearing that speech, even if minded to it before; for this better man have I sought my life long. Therefore show him to me an it please you."

"That will I right soon," quoth Robin, planting his feet sturdily apart.   "I'll show you right Nottingham play."

And with that Robin Hood drew a broad goose-wing arrow from his quiver, and set it to the string of his bow; then aimed the shaft full at the big fellow's breast.   But the other merely laughed in scorn.

"I'll tan your hide for you, if you offer to loose that string," he said quietly.

"You prate like an ass," said Robin.   "For were I but to bend my bow I could send a shaft through your heart before you could strike a single blow."

"You talk like a coward," retorted the stranger.   "You are well armed with a long bow, while I have nought but a staff in my hand."

"I scorn the name of coward," said Robin, beginning to feel ashamed of himself.   "I'll lay by my long bow and fight you on even terms.   Bide you here a little while till I cut me a cudgel like unto that you have been twiddling in your fingers."   So saying he sought his own bank again with a leap, laid aside his long bow and arrows, and cut him a stout staff of oak, straight, knotless, and a good six feet in length. But still it was a full foot shorter than his opponent's. Then back came he boldly.

"I mind not telling you, fellow," said he, "that a bout with archery would have been an easier way with me. But there are other tunes in England besides that the arrow sings." Here he whirred the staff about his head by way of practice. "So make you ready for the tune I am about to play upon your ribs. Have at you! One, two——"

"Three!" roared the giant, smiting at him instantly.

Well was it for Robin that he was quick and nimble of foot; for the blow that grazed a hair's breadth from his shoulder would have felled an ox. Nevertheless while swerving to avoid this stroke, Robin was poising for his own, and back came he forthwith—whack!

Whack! parried the other.

Whack! whack! whack! whack!

The fight waxed fast and furious. It was strength pitted against sublety and the match was a merry one. The mighty blows of the stranger went whistling around Robin's ducking head, while his own swift undercuts were fain to give the other an attack of indigestion. Yet each stood firmly in his place not moving backward or forward a foot for a good half hour, nor thinking of crying "Enough!" though some chance blow seemed likely to knock one or the other off the narrow foot-bridge. The giant's face was getting red and his breath came snorting forth like a bull's. He stepped forward with a furious onslaught to finish this audacious fellow. Robin dodged his blows lightly, then sprang in swiftly and unexpectedly and dealt the stranger such a blow upon the short ribs that you would have sworn the tanner was trimming down his hides for market.

The stranger reeled and came within an ace of falling, but regained his footing right quickly.

"By my life, you can hit hard!" he gasped forth, giving back a blow almost while he was yet staggering.

This blow was a lucky one. It caught Robin off his guard. His stick had rested a moment while he looked to see the giant topple into the water, when down came the other upon his head, whack! Robin saw more stars in that one moment than all the astronomers have since discovered, and forthwith he dropped neatly into the stream.

The cool rushing current quickly brought him to his senses, howbeit he was still so dazed that he groped blindly for the swaying reeds to pull himself up on the bank. His assailant could not forbear laughing heartily at his plight, but was also quick to lend his aid. He thrust down his long staff to Robin crying, "Lay hold of that, an your fists whirl not so much as your head!"

Robin laid hold and was hauled to dry land for all the world like a fish, except that the fish would never have come forth so wet and dripping. He lay upon the warm bank for a space to regain his senses. Then he sat up and gravely rubbed his pate.

"By all the saints!" said he, "you hit full stoutly. My head hums like a hive of bees on a summer morning."

Then he seized his horn, which lay near, and blew thereon three shrill notes that echoed against the trees. A moment of silence ensued, and then was heard the rustling of leaves and crackling of twigs like the coming of many men; and forth from the glade burst a score or two of stalwart yeomen, all clad in Lincoln green, like Robin, with good Will Stutely and the widow's three sons at their head. "Good master," cried Will Stutely, "how is this? In sooth there is not a dry thread on your body."

"Why, marry," replied Robin, "this fellow would not let me pass the foot-bridge, and when I tickled him in the ribs, he must needs answer by a pat on the head which landed me overboard."

"Then shall he taste some of his own porridge," quoth Will. "Seize him, lads! He shall have a proper ducking!"

"Nay, let him go free," said Robin. "He's a stout fellow. Forbear, the fight was a fair one and I abide by it. I surmise you also are quits?" he continued, turning to the stranger with a twinkling eye.

"I am content," said the other, "for verily you now have the best end of the cudgel. Wherefore, I like you well, and would fain know your name."

"Why," said Robin, "my men and even the Sheriff of Nottingham know me as Robin Hood, the outlaw."

"Then am I right sorry that I beat you," exclaimed the man, "for I was on my way to seek you and to try to join your merry company. But after my unmannerly use of the cudgel, I fear we are still strangers."

"Nay, never say it!" cried Robin, "I am glad I fell in with you; though, sooth to say, I did all the falling!"

And amid a general laugh the two men clasped hands, and in that clasp the strong friendship of a lifetime was begun.

"But you have not yet told us your name," said Robin, bethinking himself.

"Whence I came, men call me John Little. An you will let me join your band, ne'er doubt me, I'll play my part."

"Enter our company then, John Little; enter and welcome. The rites are few, the fee is large. We ask your whole mind and body and heart even unto death."

"I give the bond, upon my life," said he.

Thereupon Will Stutely, who loved a good jest, spoke up and said: "The infant in our household must be christened, and I'll stand godfather. This fair little stranger is so small of bone and sinew, that his old name is not to the purpose." Here he paused long enough to fill a horn in the stream. "Hark ye, my son"—standing on tiptoe to splash the water on the giant—"take your new name on entering the forest. I christen you Little John."

At this jest the men roared long and loud.

"Give him a bow, and find a full sheath of arrows for Little John," said Robin joyfully. "Can you shoot as well as fence with the staff, my friend?"

"I have hit an ash twig at forty yards," said Little John.

Thus chatting pleasantly the band turned back into the woodland and sought their secluded dell, where the trees were the thickest, the moss was the softest, and a secret path led to a cave, at once a retreat and a stronghold. Here under a mighty oak they found the rest of the band, some of whom had come in with a brace of fat does. And

here they built a ruddy fire and sat down to the meat and
ale, Robin Hood in the centre with Will Stutely on the one
hand and Little John on the other. And Robin was right
well pleased with the day's adventure, even though he had
got a drubbing; for sore ribs and heads will heal, and 'tis
not every day that one can find a recruit as stout of bone
and true of soul as Little John.

III

how Robin Hood Turned Butcher, and Entered the Sheriff's Service

The butcher he answered jolly Robin,
"No matter where I do dwell,
For a butcher am I, and to
    Nottingham
Am I going, my flesh to sell."

THE next morning the weather had turned ill and Robin Hood's band stayed close to their dry and friendly cave. The third day brought a diversion in the shape of a trap by a roving party of the Sheriff's men. A fine stag had been struck down by one of Will Stutely's fellows, and he and others had stepped forth from the covert to seize it, when twenty bowmen from Nottingham appeared at the end of the glade. Down dropped Will's men on all fours, barely in time to hear a shower of arrows whistle above their heads. Then from behind the friendly trees they sent back such a welcome that the Sheriff's men deemed it prudent not to tarry in their steps. Two of them, in sooth, bore back unpleasant wounds in their shoulders, from the encounter.

39

When they returned to town the Sheriff waxed red with rage.

"What," he gasped, "do my men fear to fight this Robin Hood, face to face? Would that *I* could get him within my reach, once. We should see then; we should see!"

What it was the Sheriff would see, he did not state. But he was to have his wish granted in short space, and you and I will see how he profited by it.

The fourth day and the one following this friendly bout, Little John was missing. One of the men said that he saw him talking with a beggar, but did not know whither they had gone. Two more days passed. Robin grew uneasy. He did not doubt the faith of Little John, but he was fearful lest a roving band of Foresters had captured him.

At last Robin could not remain quiet. Up sprang he, with bow and arrows, and a short sword at his side.

"I must away to Nottingham town, my men," he cried. "The goodly Sheriff has long desired to see me; and mayhap he can tell me tidings of the best quarter-staff in the shire"—meaning Little John.

Others of the band besought him to let them go with him, but he would not.

"Nay," he said smilingly, "the Sheriff and I are too good friends to put doubt upon our meeting. But tarry ye in the edge of the wood opposite the west gate of the town, and ye may be of service ere to-morrow night."

So saying he strode forward to the road leading to Nottingham, and stood as before looking up and down to see if the way was clear. Back at a bend in the road he heard a rumbling and a lumbering, when up drove a stout butcher, whistling gayly, and driving a mare that sped slowly enough because of the weight of meat with which the cart was loaded.

"A good morrow to you, friend," hailed Robin. "Whence come you and where go you with your load of meat?"

"A good morrow to you," returned the butcher, civilly enough. "No matter where I dwell. I am but a simple butcher, and to Nottingham am I going, my flesh to sell. 'Tis Fair week, and my beef and mutton should fetch a fair penny," and he laughed loudly at his jest. "But whence come you?"

"A yeoman am I, from Lockesley town. Men call me Robin Hood."

"The saints forefend that you should treat me ill!" said the butcher in terror. "Oft have I heard of you, and how you lighten the purses of the fat priests and knights. But I am naught but a poor butcher, selling this load of meat, perchance, for enough to pay my quarter's rent."

"Rest you, my friend, rest you," quoth Robin, "not so much as a silver penny would I take from you, for I love an honest Saxon face and a fair name with my neighbors. But I would strike a bargain with you."

Here he took from his girdle a well-filled purse, and continued, "I would fain be a butcher, this day, and sell meat at Nottingham town. Could you sell me your meat, your cart, your mare, and your good-will, without loss, for four marks?"

"Heaven bless ye, good Robin," cried the butcher right joyfully, "that can I!" And he leaped down forthwith from the cart, and handed Robin the reins in exchange for the purse.

"One moment more," laughed Robin, "we must e'en change garments for the nonce. Take mine and scurry home quickly lest the King's Foresters try to put a hole through this Lincoln green."

So saying he donned the butcher's blouse and apron, and, climbing into the cart, drove merrily down the road to the town.

When he came to Nottingham he greeted the scowling gate-keeper blithely and proceeded to the market-place. Boldly he led his shuffling horse to the place where the butchers had their stalls. He had no notion of the price to ask for his meat, but put on a foolish and simple air as he called aloud his wares:—

> "Hark ye, lasses and dames, hark ye,
> Good meat come buy, come buy,
> Three pen'orths go for one penny,
> And a kiss is good, say I!"

Now when the folk found what a simple butcher he was, they crowded around his cart; for he really did sell three times as much for one penny as was sold by the other butchers. And one or two serving-lasses with twinkling eyes liked his comely face so well that they willingly gave boot of a kiss.

But the other butchers were wroth when they found how he was taking their trade; and they accordingly put their heads together.

One said, "He is a prodigal and has sold his father's land, and this is his first venture in trading."

Another said, "He is a thief who has murdered a butcher and stolen his horse and meat."

Robin heard these sayings, but only laughed merrily and sang his song the louder. His good humor made the people laugh also and crowd round his cart closely, shouting uproariously when some buxom lass submitted to be kissed.

Then the butchers saw that they must meet craft with craft; and they said to him, "Come, brother butcher, if

Louis Slobodkin

you would sell meat with us, you must e'en join our guild
and stand by the rules of our trade."

"We dine at the Sheriff's mansion to-day," said another,
"and you must make one of our party."

> "Accurst of his heart," said jolly Robin
> "That a butcher doth deny.
> I'll go with you, my brethren true,
> And as fast as I can hie."

Whereupon, having sold all his meat, he left his horse
and cart in charge of a friendly hostler and prepared to
follow his mates to the Mansion House.

It was the Sheriff's custom to dine various guilds of the
trade, from time to time, on Fair days, for he got a pretty
profit out of the fees they paid him for the right to trade in
the market-place. The Sheriff was already come with
great pomp into the banqueting room, when Robin Hood
and three or four butchers entered, and he greeted them
all with great condescension; and presently the whole of
a large company was seated at a table groaning beneath
the good cheer of the feast.

Now the Sheriff bade Robin sit by his right hand, at the
head of the board; for one or two butchers had whispered
to the official, "That fellow is a right mad blade, who yet
made us much sport to-day. He sold more meat for one
penny that we could sell for three; and he gave extra
weight to whatsoever lass would buss him." And others
said, "He is some prodigal who knows not the value of
goods, and may be plucked by a shrewd man right closely."

The Sheriff was willing to pluck a prodigal with the next
man, and he was moreover glad to have a guest who promised to enliven the feast. So, as I have told you, he placed
Robin by his side, and he made much of him and laughed

boisterously at his jests; though sooth to say, the laugh were come by easily, for Robin had never been in a merrier mood, and his quips and jests soon put the whole table at a roar.

Then my lord Bishop of Hereford came in, last of all, to say a ponderous grace and take his seat on the other side of the Sheriff—the prelate's fat body showing up in goodly contrast to the other's lean bones.

After grace was said, and while the servants clattered in with the meat platters, Robin stood up and said:

"An amen say I to my lord Bishop's thanks! How, now, my fine fellows, be merry and drink deep; for the shot I'll pay ere I go my way, though it cost me five pounds and more. So my lords and gentlemen all, spare not the wine, but fall to lustily."

"Hear! hear!" shouted the butchers.

"Now are you a right jolly soul," quoth the Sheriff, "but this feast is mine own. Howbeit you must have many a head of horned beasts, and many an acre of broad land, to spend from your purse so freely."

"Aye, that have I," returned Robin, his eyes all a twinkle, "five hundred horned beasts have I and my brothers, and none of them have we been able to sell. That is why I have turned butcher. But I know not the trade, and would gladly sell the whole herd, an I could find a buyer."

At this, the Sheriff's greed 'gan to rise. Since this fool *would* be plucked, thought he, why should not he do the plucking?

"Five hundred beasts, say you?" he queried sharply.

"Five hundred and ten fat beasts by actual count, that I would sell for a just figure. Aye, to him who will pay me in right money, would I sell them for twenty pieces of gold. Is that too much to ask, lording?"

Was there ever such an idiot butcher? thought the
Sheriff; and he so far forgot his dignity as to nudge the
Bishop in the fat ribs.

"Nay, good fellow," quoth he chuckling, "I am always
ready to help any in my shire. An you cannot find a buyer
for your herd at this just figure, I will e'en buy them
myself."

At this generosity Robin was quite overcome, and fell
to praising the Sheriff to the skies, and telling him that he
should not have cause to forget the kindness.

"Tut, tut," said the Sheriff, " 'tis naught but a trade.
Drive in your herd to-morrow to the market-place and you
shall have money down."

"Nay, excellence," said Robin, "that can I not easily do,
for they are grazing in scattered fashion. But they are
over near Gamewell, not more than a mile therefrom at

most. Will you not come and choose your own beasts
to-morrow?"

"Aye, that I will," said the Sheriff, his cupidity casting
his caution to the winds. "Tarry with me over night, and
I will go with you in the morning."

This was a poser for Robin, since he liked not the idea
of staying over night at the Sheriff's house. He had hoped
to appoint a meeting-place for the other, but now saw

that this might excite doubt. He looked around at the company. By this time, you must know, the feast had progressed far, and the butchers were deep in their cups. The Sheriff and Robin had talked in a low voice, and my lord Bishop was almost asleep.

"Agreed," said Robin presently, and the words were no sooner out of his mouth than the door opened and a serving-man entered bearing a tray of mulled wine. At sight of the fellow's face, Robin gave an involuntary start of surprise which was instantly checked. The other also saw him, stood still a moment, and, as if forgetting something, turned about and left the hall.

It was Little John.

A dozen questions flashed across Robin's mind, and he could find answer for none of them. What was Little John doing in the Sheriff's house? Why had he not told the band? Was he true to them? Would he betray him?

But these questions of distrust were dismissed from Robin's open mind as soon as they had entered. He knew that Little John was faithful and true.

He recovered his spirits and began again upon a vein of foolish banter, for the amusement of the Sheriff and his guests, all being now merry with wine.

"A song!" one of them shouted, and the cry was taken up round the table. Robin mounted his chair and trolled forth:

"A lass and a butcher of Nottingham
    Agreed 'twixt them for to wed:
Says he, 'I'll give ye the meat, fair dame,
    An ye will give me the bread.'"

Then they joined in the chorus amid a pounding of cups upon the board:

"With a hey and a ho
And a hey nonny no,
A butcher of Nottingham!"

While the song was at its height, Little John reappeared, with other servants, and refilled the cups. He came up to Robin and, as if asking him if he would have more wine, said softly, "Meet me in the pantry to-night."

Robin nodded, and sang loudly. The day was already far spent, and presently the company broke up with many hiccupy bows to the Sheriff and little notice of the drowsy Bishop.

When the company was dispersed, the Sheriff bade a servant show Robin to his room, and promised to see him at breakfast the next day.

Robin kept his word and met Little John that night, and the Sheriff next day; but Little John has been doing so much in the meantime that he must be allowed a chapter to himself.

So let us turn to another story that was sung of, in the ballads of olden time, and find out how Little John entered the Sheriff's service.

IV

how Little John Entered the Sheriff's Service

List and hearken, gentlemen,
All ye that now be here,
Of little John, that was Knight's-man,
Good mirth ye now shall hear.

I⊤ had come around another Fair day at Nottingham town, and folk crowded there by all the gates. Goods of many kinds were displayed in gaily colored booths, and at every cross-street a free show was in progress. Here and there, stages had been erected for the play at quarter-staff, a highly popular sport.

There was a fellow, one Eric of Lincoln, who was thought to be the finest man with the staff for miles around. His feats were sung about in ballads through all the shire. A great boaster was he withal, and to-day he strutted about on one of these corner stages, and vaunted of his prowess, and offered to crack any man's crown for a shilling. Several had tried their skill with Eric, but he had soon sent them spinning in no gentle manner, amid the jeers and laughter of the onlookers.

A beggar-man sat over against Eric's stage and grinned every time a pate was cracked. He was an uncouth fel-

50

low, ragged and dirty and unshaven. Eric caught sight of his leering face at one of his boasts—for there was a lull in the game, because no man else wanted to come within reach of Eric's blows. Eric, I say, noticed the beggar-man grinning at him rather impudently, and turned toward him sharply.

"How now, you dirty villain!" quoth he, "mend your manners to your betters, or, by our Lady, I'll dust your rags for you."

The beggar-man still grinned. "I am always ready to mend my manners to my *betters*," said he, "but I am afraid *you* cannot teach me any better than you can dust my jacket."

"Come up! Come up!" roared the other, flourishing his staff.

"That will I," said the beggar, getting up slowly and with difficulty. "It will pleasure me hugely to take a braggart down a notch, an some good man will lend me a stout quarter-staff."

At this a score of idlers reached him their staves—being ready enough to see another man have his head cracked, even if they wished to save their own—and he took the stoutest and heaviest of all. He made a sorry enough figure as he climbed awkwardly upon the stage, but when he had gained it, he towered full half a head above the other, for all his awkwardness. Nathless, he held his stick so clumsily that the crowd laughed in great glee.

Now each man took his place and looked the other up and down, watching warily for an opening. Only a moment stood they thus, for Eric, intent on teaching this rash beggar a lesson and sweeping him speedily off the stage, launched forth boldly and gave the other a sounding crack on the shoulder. The beggar danced about, and made as

though he would drop his staff from very pain, while the
crowd roared and Eric raised himself for another crushing
blow.   But just then the awkward beggar came to life.
Straightening himself like a flash he dealt Eric a back-
handed blow, the like of which he had never before seen.
Down went the boaster to the floor with a sounding
thump, and the fickle people yelled and laughed themselves purple; for it was a new sight to see Eric of Lincoln
eating dust.

Louis Slobodkin

But he was up again almost as soon as he had fallen, and right quickly retreated to his own ringside to gather his wits and watch for an opening. He saw instantly that he had no easy antagonist, and he came in cautiously this time.

And now those who stood around saw the merriest game of quarter-staff that was ever played inside the walls of Nottingham town. Both men were on their guard and

fenced with fine skill, being well matched in prowess.
Again and again did Eric seek to force an opening under
the other's guard, and just as often were his blows parried.
The beggar stood sturdily in his tracks contenting himself
with beating off the attack. For a long time their blows
met like the steady crackling of some huge forest fire, and
Eric strove to be wary, for he now knew that the other had
no mean wits or mettle. But he grew right mad at last,
and began to send down blows so fierce and fast that you
would have sworn a great hail-storm was pounding on the
shingles over your head. Yet he never so much as entered
the tall beggar's guard.

Then at last the stranger saw his chance and changed
his tune of fighting. With one upward stroke he sent
Eric's staff whirling through the air. With another he
tapped Eric on the head; and, with a third broad swing,
ere the other could recover himself, he swept him clear
off the stage, much as you would brush a fly off the window
pane.

Now the people danced and shouted and made so much
ado that the shop-keepers left their stalls and others came
running from every direction. The victory of the queer
beggar made him immensely popular. Eric had been a
great bully, and many had suffered defeat and insult at his
hand. So the ragged stranger found money and food and
drink everywhere at his disposal, and he feasted right
comfortably till the afternoon.

Then a long-bow contest came on, and to it the beggar
went with some of his new friends. It was held in the
same arena that Robin had formerly entered; and again
the Sheriff and lords and ladies graced the scene with their
presence, while the people crowded to their places.

When the archers had stepped forward, the herald rose

and proclaimed the rules of the game: how that each man
should shoot three shots, and to him who shot best the
prize of a yoke of fat steers should belong. A dozen keen-
eyed bow-men were there, and among them some of the
best fellows in the Forester's and Sheriff's companies.
Down at the end of the line towered the tall beggar-man,
who must needs twang a bow-string with the best of them.

The Sheriff noted his queer figure and asked: "Who is
that ragged fellow?"

" 'Tis he that hath but now so soundly cracked the
crown of Eric of Lincoln," was the reply.

The shooting presently began, and the targets soon
showed a fine reckoning. Last of all came the beggar's
turn.

"By your leave," he said loudly, "I'd like it well to shoot
with any other man here present at a mark of my own placing." And he strode down the lists with a slender peeled
sapling which he stuck upright in the ground. "There,"
said he, "is a right good mark. Will any man try it?"

But not an archer would risk his reputation on so small
a target. Whereupon the beggar drew his bow with seeming carelessness and split the wand with his shaft.

"Long live the beggar!" yelled the bystanders.

The Sheriff swore a full great oath, and said: "This man
is the best archer that ever yet I saw." And he beckoned
to him, and asked him: "How now, good fellow, what is
your name, and in what country were you born?"

"In Holderness I was born," the man replied; "men call
me Reynold Greenleaf."

"You are a sturdy fellow, Reynold Greenleaf, and de-
serve better apparel than that you wear at present. Will
you enter my service? I will give you twenty marks a
year, above your living, and three good suits of clothes."

"Three good suits, say you? Then right gladly will I enter your service, for my back has been bare this many a long day."

Then Reynold turned him about to the crowd and shouted: "Hark ye, good people, I have entered the Sheriff's service, and need not the yoke of steers for prize. So take them for yourselves, to feast withal."

At this the crowd shouted more merrily than ever, and threw their caps high into the air. And none so popular a man had come to Nottingham town in many a long day as this same Reynold Greenleaf.

Now you may have guessed, by this time, who Reynold Greenleaf really was; so I shall tell you that he was none other than Little John. And forth went he to the Sheriff's house, and entered his service. But it was a sorry day for the Sheriff when he got his new man. For Little John winked his shrewd eye and said softly to himself: "By my faith, I shall be the worst servant to him that ever yet had he!"

Two days passed by. Little John, it must be confessed, did not make a good servant. He insisted upon eating the Sheriff's best bread and drinking his best wine, so that the steward waxed wroth. Nathless the Sheriff held him in high esteem, and made great talk of taking him along on the next hunting trip.

It was now the day of the banquet to the butchers, about which we have already heard. The banquet hall, you must know, was not in the main house, but connected with it by a corridor. All the servants were bustling about making preparations for the feast, save only Little John, who must needs lie abed the greater part of the day. But he presented himself at last, when the dinner was half over;

and being desirous of seeing the guests for himself he went into the hall with the other servants to pass the wine. First, however, I am afraid that some of the wine passed his own lips while he went down the corridor.

When he entered the banqueting hall, whom should he see but Robin Hood himself. We can imagine the start of surprise felt by each of these bold fellows upon seeing the other in such strange company. But they kept their secrets, as we have seen, and arranged to meet each other that same night. Meanwhile, the proud Sheriff little knew that he harbored the two chief outlaws of the whole countryside beneath his roof.

After the feast was over and night was beginning to advance, Little John felt faint of stomach and remembered him that he had eaten nothing all that day. Back went he to the pantry to see what eatables were laid by. But there, locking up the stores for the night, stood the fat steward.

"Good Sir Steward," said Little John, "give me to dine for it is long for Greenleaf to be fasting."

The steward looked grimly at him and rattled the keys at his girdle.

"Sirrah lie-abed," quoth he, "'tis late in the day to be talking of eating. Since you have waited thus long to be hungry, you can e'en take your appetite back to bed again."

"Now by mine appetite that will I not do," cried Little John. "Your own paunch of fat would be enough for any bear to sleep on through the winter. But my stomach craves food, and food it shall have!"

Saying this he brushed past the steward and tried the door, but it was locked fast; whereat the fat steward chuckled and jangled his keys again.

Then was Little John right mad, and he brought down

his huge fist on the door-panel with a sledge-hammer blow
that shivered an opening you could thrust your hand into.
Little John stooped and peered through the hole to see
what food lay within reach, when crack! went the steward's keys upon his crown, and that worthy danced around
him playing a tattoo that made Little John's ears ring. At
this he turned upon the steward and gave him such a rap
that his back went nigh in two, and over went the fat
fellow rolling on the floor.

"Lie there," quoth Little John, "till ye find strength to
go to bed. Meanwhile, I must be about my dinner." And
he kicked open the buttery door without ceremony and
brought to light a venison pasty and cold roast pheasant—
goodly sights to a hungry man. Placing these down on a
convenient shelf he fell to with right good will. So Little
John ate and drank as much as he would.

Now the Sheriff had in his kitchen a cook, a stout man
and bold, who heard the rumpus and came in to see how
the land lay. There stood Little John leaning comfortably
against the sideboard and eating away for dear life, while
the fat steward was rolled under the table like a bundle
of rags.

"I make my vow!" said the cook, "you are a shrewd hind
to dwell thus in a household, and ask thus to dine." So
saying he laid aside his spit and drew a good sword that
hung at his side.

"I make my vow!" said Little John, "you are a bold man
and hardy to come thus between me and my meat. So defend yourself and see that you prove the better man."
And he drew his own sword and crossed weapons with
the cook.

Then back and forth they clashed with sullen sound.
The old ballad which tells of their fight says that they

thought nothing for to flee, but stiffly for to stand. There
they fought sore together, two miles away and more, but
neither might the other harm for the space of a full hour.

"I make my vow!" cried Little John, "you are the best
swordsman that ever yet I saw. What say you to resting
a space and eating and drinking good health with me.
Then we may fall to again with the swords."

"Agreed!" said the cook, who loved good fare as well as
a good fight; and they both laid by their swords and fell to
the food with hearty will. The venison pasty soon disappeared, and the roast pheasant flew at as lively a rate as
ever the bird itself had sped. Then the warriors rested a
space and patted their stomachs, and smiled across at each
other like bosom friends; for a man when he has dined
looks out pleasantly upon the world.

"And now good Reynold Greenleaf," said the cook, "we
may as well settle this brave fight we have in hand."

"A true saying," rejoined the other, "but first tell me,
friend,—for I protest you are my friend henceforth—what
is the score we have to settle?"

"Naught save who can handle the sword best," said the
cook. "By my troth I had thought to carve you like a
capon ere now."

"And I had long since thought to shave your ears," replied Little John. "This bout we can settle in right good
time. But just now I and my master have need of you, and
you can turn your stout blade to better service than that
of the Sheriff."

"Whose service would that be?" asked the cook.

"Mine," answered a would-be butcher entering the
room, "and I am Robin Hood."

V

hOW The Sheriff Lost Three Good Servants and Found Them Again

"Make good cheer," said Robin Hood.
"Sheriff! for charity!
And for the love of Little John
Thy life is granted thee!"

THE cook gasped in amazement. This Robin Hood! and under the Sheriff's very roof!

"Now by my troth you are a brave fellow," he said. "I have heard great tales of your prowess, and the half has not been told. But who might this tall slasher be?"

"Men do call me Little John, good fellow."

"Then Little John, or Reynold Greenleaf, I like you well, on my honor as Much the miller's son; and you too, bold Robin Hood. An you take me, I will enter your service right gladly."

"Spoken like a stout man!" said Robin, seizing him by the hand. "But I must back to my own bed, lest some sleepy warden stumble upon me, and I be forced to run him

61

through. Lucky for you twain that wine flowed so freely in this house to-day; else the noise of your combat would have brought other onlookers besides Robin Hood. Now if ye would flee the house to-night, I will join you in the good greenwood to-morrow."

"But, good master," said the cook, "you would not stay here over night! Verily, it is running your head into a noose. Come with us. The Sheriff has set strict watch on all the gates, since 'tis Fair week, but I know the warden at the west gate and could bring us through safely. To-morrow you will be stayed."

"Nay, that will I not," laughed Robin, "for I shall go through with no less escort than the Sheriff himself. Now do you, Little John, and do you, Much the miller's son, go right speedily. In the borders of the wood you will find my merry men. Tell them to kill two fine harts against to-morrow eve, for we shall have great company and lordly sport."

And Robin left them as suddenly as he had come.

"Comrade," then said Little John, "we may as well bid the Sheriff's roof farewell. But ere we go, it would seem a true pity to fail to take such of the Sheriff's silver plate as will cause us to remember him, and also grace our special feasts."

" 'Tis well said indeed," quoth the cook.

Thereupon they got a great sack and filled it with silver plate from the shelves where it would not at once be missed, and they swung the sack between them, and away they went, out of the house, out of the town, and into the friendly shelter of Sherwood Forest.

The next morning the servants were late astir in the Sheriff's house. The steward awoke from a heavy sleep, but his cracked head was still in such a whirl that he could not have sworn whether the Sheriff had ever owned so much as one silver dish. So the theft went undiscovered for the nonce.

Robin Hood met the Sheriff at breakfast, when his host soon spoke of what was uppermost in his heart—the purchase of that fine herd of cattle near Gamewell. 'Twas clear that a vision of them, purchased for twenty paltry gold pieces, had been with him all through the night, in his dreams. And Robin again appeared such a silly fellow that the Sheriff saw no need of dissembling, but said that he was ready to start at once to look at the herd.

Accordingly they set forth, Robin astride a black horse from the Sheriff's stables, and the Sheriff himself mounted on a spirited brown one. For he wanted to lose no time in striking a bargain with this silly fellow. Out of Nottingham town, through gates open wide, they proceeded, and took the hill road leading through Sherwood Forest. And as they went on and plunged deeper among the trees, Robin whistled blithely and sang snatches of tunes.

"Why are you so gay, fellow?" said the Sheriff, for, sooth to say, the silence of the woods was making him uneasy.

"I am whistling to keep my courage up," replied Robin.

"What is there to fear, when you have the Sheriff of Nottingham beside you?" quoth the other pompously.

Robin scratched his head.

"They do say that Robin Hood and his men care little for the Sheriff," he said.

"Pooh!" said the Sheriff. "I would not give *that* for their lives, if I could only lay hands upon them." And he snapped his fingers angrily.

"But Robin Hood himself was on this very road the last time I came to town," said the other.

The Sheriff started at the crackling of a twig under his
horse's feet and looked around.

"Did you see him?" he asked.

"Aye, that did I!   He wanted the use of my mare and

cart to drive to Nottingham.   He said he would fain turn
butcher.   But see!"

As he spoke he came to a turn in the road, and there before them stood a herd of the King's deer, feeding.   Robin
pointed to them and continued:

"There is my herd of cattle, good Master Sheriff!   How
do you like them?   Are they not fat and fair to see?"

The Sheriff drew rein quickly.   "Now fellow," quoth he,
"I would I were well out of this forest, for I care not to see
such herds as these, or such faces as yours.   Choose your
own way, therefore, whoever you be, and let me go mine."

"Nay," laughed Robin, seizing the Sheriff's bridle, "I
have been at too much pains to cultivate your company to
forego it now so easily.   Besides, I wish you to meet some

of my friends and dine with me, since you have so lately entertained me at your board."

So saying he clapped a horn to his lips and winded three merry notes. The deer bounded away; and before the last of them was seen, there came a running and a rustling, and out from behind covert and tree came full twoscore of men, clad in Lincoln green, and bearing good yew bows in their hands and short swords at their sides. Up they ran to Robin Hood and doffed their caps to him respectfully, while the Sheriff sat still from very amazement.

"Welcome to the greenwood!" said one of the leaders, bending the knee with mock reverence before the Sheriff.

The Sheriff glared. It was Little John.

"Woe the worth, Reynold Greenleaf," he said, "you have betrayed me!"

"I make my vow," said Little John, "that you are to blame, master. I was misserved of my dinner, when I was at your house. But we shall set you down to a feast we hope you will enjoy."

"Well spoken, Little John," said Robin Hood. "Take you his bridle and let us do honor to the guest who has come to feast with us."

Then turning abruptly the whole company plunged into the heart of the forest.

After twisting and turning till the Sheriff's bewildered head sat dizzily upon his shoulders, the greenwood men passed through a narrow alley amid the trees which led to a goodly open space flanked by wide-spreading oaks. Under the largest of these a pleasant fire was crackling, and near it two fine harts lay ready for cooking. Around the blaze were gathered another company of yeomen quite as large as that which came with Robin Hood. Up sprang they as the latter advanced and saluted their leader with deference, but with hearty gladness to see him back again.

The merry wag Will Stutely was in command; and when he saw the pale-faced Sheriff being led in like a culprit, he took his cloak and laid it humbly upon the ground and besought the Sheriff to alight upon it, as the ground of Sherwood was unused to such dignitaries.

"Bestir yourselves, good fellows!" cried Robin Hood; "and while our new cook, whom I see with us, is preparing a feast worthy of our high guest, let us have a few games to do him honor!"

Then while the whole glade was filled with the savory smell of roasting venison and fat capons, and brown pasties warmed beside the blaze, and mulled wine sent forth a cordial fragrance, Robin Hood placed the Sheriff upon a knoll beneath the largest oak and sat himself down by him.

First stepped forward several pairs of men armed with the quarter-staff, the widow's sons among them, and so skilfully did they thrust and parry and beat down guards, that the Sheriff, who loved a good game as well as any man, clapped his hands, forgetting where he was, and shouted, "Well struck! well struck! Never have I seen such blows at all the Fairs of Nottingham!"

Then the best archers of the band set up a small wand at eightscore paces distant, and thereon they affixed a wreath of green. And the archers began to shoot; and he who shot not through the garland without disturbing its leaves and tendrils was fain to submit to a good sound buffet from Little John. But right cunning was the shooting, for the men had spent a certain time in daily practice, and many were the shafts which sped daintily through the circle. Nathless now and again some luckless fellow would shoot awry and would be sent winding from a long arm blow from the tall lieutenant while the glade roared with laughter. And none more hearty a guffaw was given than came from the Sheriff's own throat, for the spirit of the greenwood was upon him.

But presently his high mood was dashed. The company sat down to meat, and the guest was treated to two more disturbing surprises. The cook came forward to serve the food, when the Sheriff beheld in him his own former servant, and one whom he supposed was at that moment in the scullery at Nottingham.

Much the miller's son grinned by way of answer to the Sheriff's amazement, and served the plates, and placed them before the party. Then did the Sheriff gasp and fairly choke with rage. The service was his own silverware from the Mansion House!

"You rascals! you rogues!" he spluttered. "Was it not enough to defraud me out of three of my servants, that you must also rob me of my best silver service? Nay, by my life, but I will not touch your food!"

But Robin Hood bade him pause.

"Gramercy!" quoth he, "servants come and go, in merry England, and so does service. The platters are but used to do your worship honor. And as for your life, it is forfeit to your eagerness to buy my herd of cattle so cheaply. Now sit you down again and make good cheer, Sheriff, for charity! And for the love of Little John your life is granted you!"

So the Sheriff sat him down again with the best face he could assume, and soon the cook's viands were disappearing down his gullet as rapidly as the next man's. And they feasted royally and clinked each other's cups until the sun had ceased to print the pattern of the leaves upon the forest carpet.

Then the Sheriff arose and said: "I thank you, Robin Hood, one-time butcher, and you, Little John, one-time beggar, and you, Much, one-time cook, and all you good men who have entertained me in Sherwood so well. Promises I make not as to how I shall requite you when next you come to Nottingham, for I am in the King's service. So for the present the score rests with you. But the shadows grow long and I must away, if you will be pleased to pilot me to the road."

Then Robin Hood and all his men arose and drank the Sheriff's health, and Robin said: "If you must needs go at once we will not detain you—except that you have forgotten two things."

"What may they be?" asked the Sheriff, while his heart sank within him.

"You forget that you came with me to-day to buy a herd of horned beasts; likewise that he who dines at the Greenwood Inn must pay the landlord."

The Sheriff fidgetted like a small boy who has forgotten his lesson.

"Nay, I have but a small sum with me," he began apologetically.

"What is that sum, gossip?" questioned Little John, "for my own wage should also come out of it!"

"And mine!" said Much.

"And mine!" smiled Robin.

The Sheriff caught his breath. "By my troth, are all these silver dishes worth anything?"

The outlaws roared heartily at this.

"I'll tell you what it is, worship," said Robin, "we three rascally servants will compound our back wages for those plates. And we will keep the herd of cattle free for our own use—and the King's. But this little tavern bill should be settled! Now, what sum have you about you?"

"I have only those twenty pieces of gold, and twenty others," said the Sheriff: and well it was that he told the truth for once, for Robin said:

"Count it."

Little John turned the Sheriff's wallet inside out, and the outlaws counted the booty. " 'Tis true enough," he said.

"Then you shall pay no more than twenty pieces for your entertainment, excellence," decreed Robin. "Speak I soothly, men of greenwood?"

"Good!" echoed the others.

"The Sheriff should swear by his patron saint that he will not molest us," said Will Stutely; and this addition was carried unanimously.

"So be it, then," cried Little John, approaching the Sheriff. "Now swear by your life and your patron saint——"

"I will swear it by St. George, who is patron of us all," said the Sheriff vigorously, "that I will never disturb or distress the outlaws in Sherwood."

"But let me catch any of you *out* of Sherwood!" thought he to himself.

Then the twenty pieces of gold were paid over, and the Sheriff once more prepared to depart.

"Never had we so worshipful a guest before," said Robin; "and as the new moon is beginning to silver the leaves, I shall bear you company myself for part of the way. 'Twas I who brought you into the wood."

"Nay, I protest against your going needlessly far," said the Sheriff.

"But I protest that I am loath to lose your company," replied Robin. "The next time I may not be so pleased."

And he took the Sheriff's horse by the bridle rein, and led him through the lane and by many a thicket till the main road was reached.

"Now fare you well, good Sheriff," hc said, "and whcn next you think to despoil a poor prodigal, remember the herd you would have bought over against Gamewell. And when next you employ a servant, make certain that he is not employing you."

So saying he smote the nag's haunch, and off went the Sheriff upon the road to Nottingham.

And that is how—you will find from many ballads that came to be sung at the Sheriff's expense, and which are known even to the present day,—that, I say, is how the Sheriff lost three good servants and found them again.

VI

how Robin Hood
Met Will Scarlet

The youngster was clothed in scarlet
      red,
   In scarlet fine and gay;
And he did frisk it o'er the plain,
   And chanted a roundelay.

ONE fine morning, soon after the
proud Sheriff had been brought to grief, Robin Hood and
Little John went strolling down a path through the wood.
It was not far from the foot-bridge where they had fought
their memorable battle; and by common impulse they directed their steps to the brook to quench their thirst and
rest them in the cool bushes. The morning gave promise
of a hot day. The road even by the brook was dusty. So
the cooling stream was very pleasing and grateful to their
senses.

On each side of them, beyond the dusty highway,
stretched out broad fields of tender young corn. On the
yon side of the fields uprose the sturdy oaks and beeches
and ashes of the forest; while at their feet modest violets
peeped out shyly and greeted the loiterers with an odor
which made the heart glad. Over on the far side of the
brook in a tiny bay floated three lily-pads; and from amid
some clover blossoms on the bank an industrious bee rose

with the hum of busy contentment. It was a day so brim-
ful of quiet joy that the two friends lay flat on their backs
gazing up at the scurrying clouds, and neither caring to
break the silence.

Presently they heard some one coming up the road
whistling gayly, as though he owned the whole world and
'twas but made to whistle in. Anon he chanted a roundelay with a merry note.

"By my troth, a gay bird!" quoth Robin, raising up on
his elbow. "Let us lie still, and trust that his purse is not
as light as his heart."

So they lay still, and in a minute more up came a smart
stranger dressed in scarlet and silk and wearing a jaunty
hat with a curling cock feather in it. His whole costume
was of scarlet, from the feather to the silk hosen on his
legs. A goodly sword hung at his side, its scabbard all
embossed with tilting knights and weeping ladies. His
hair was long and yellow and hung clustering about his
shoulders, for all the world like a schoolgirl's; and he bore
himself with as mincing a gait as the pertest of them.

Little John clucked his teeth drolly at this sight. "By
my troth, a gay bird!" he said, echoing the other's words—
then added, "But not so bad a build for all his prettiness.
Look you, those calves and thighs are well rounded and
straight. The arms, for all that gold-wrought cloak, hang
stoutly from full shoulders. I warrant you the fop can
use his dainty sword right well on occasion."

"Nay," retorted Robin, "he is naught but a ladies' man
from court. My long-bow 'gainst a plugged shilling that
he would run and bellow lustily at sight of a quarter-staff.
Stay you behind this bush and I will soon get some rare
sport out of him. Belike his silk purse may contain more
pennies than the law allows to one man in Sherwood or

Barnesdale." So saying Robin Hood stepped forth briskly
from the covert and planted himself in the way of the
scarlet stranger. The latter had walked so slowly that he
was scarce come to their resting-place; and now on be-
holding Robin he neither slackened nor quickened his
pace but sauntered idly straight ahead, looking to the
right and to the left, with the finest air in the world, but
never once at Robin.

"Hold!" quoth the outlaw. "What mean ye by running
thus over a wayfarer, rough shod?"

"Wherefore should I hold, good fellow?" said the
stranger in a smooth voice, and looking at Robin for the
first time.

"Because I bid you to," replied Robin.

"And who may you be?" asked the other as coolly as you
please.

"What my name is matters not," said Robin; "but know
that I am a public tax-gatherer and equalizer of shillings.
If your purse have more than a just number of shillings or
pence, I must e'en lighten it somewhat; for there are many
worthy people round about these borders who have less
than the just amount. Wherefore, sweet gentleman, I
pray you hand over your purse without more ado, that I
may judge of its weight in proper fashion."

The other smiled as sweetly as though a lady were paying him a compliment.

"You are a droll fellow," he said calmly. "Your speech
amuses me mightily. Pray continue, if you have not done,
for I am in no hurry this morning."

"I have said all with my tongue that is needful," retorted
Robin, beginning to grow red under the collar. "Nathless,
I have other arguments which may not be so pleasing to
your dainty skin. Prithee, stand and deliver. I promise
to deal fairly with the purse."

"Alack-a-day!" said the stranger with a little shrug of his shoulders; "I am deeply sorrowful that I cannot show my purse to every rough lout that asks to see it. But I really could not, as I have further need of it myself and every farthing it contains. Wherefore, pray stand aside."

"Nay that will I not! and 'twill go the harder with you if you do not yield at once."

"Good fellow," said the other gently, "have I not heard all your speech with patience? Now that is all I promised to do. My conscience is salved and I must go on my way. 'T-rol-o-rol-e-loo!' " he caroled, making as though to depart.

"Hold, I say!" quoth Robin hotly; for he knew how Little John must be chuckling at this from behind the bushes. "Hold I say, else I shall have to bloody those fair locks of yours!" And he swung his quarter-staff threateningly.

"Alas!" moaned the stranger, shaking his head. "The pity of it all! Now I shall have to run this fellow through with my sword! And I had hoped to be a peaceable man henceforth!" And sighing deeply he drew his shining blade and stood on guard.

"Put by your weapon," said Robin. "It is too pretty a piece of steel to get cracked with a common oak cudgel; and that is what would happen on the first pass I made at you. Get you a stick like mine out of yon undergrowth and we will fight fairly, man to man."

The stranger thought a moment with his usual slowness, and eyed Robin from head to foot. Then he unbuckled his scabbard, laid it and the sword aside, and walked deliberately over to the oak thicket. Choosing from among the shoots and saplings he found a stout little tree to his liking, when he laid hold of it, without stopping to cut it, and gave a tug. Up it came root and all, as though it were a stalk of corn, and the stranger walked back trimming it as quietly as though pulling up trees were the easiest thing in the world.

Little John from his hiding-place saw the feat, and could hardly restrain a long whistle. "By our Lady!" he muttered to himself, "I would not be in Master Robin's boots!"

Whatever Robin thought upon seeing the stranger's strength, he uttered not a word and budged not an inch. He only put his oak staff at parry as the other took his stand.

There was a threefold surprise that day, by the brookside. The stranger and Robin and Little John in the bushes all found a combat that upset all reckoning. The

stranger for all his easy strength and cool nerve found an
antagonist who met his blows with the skill of a woodman.
Robin found the stranger as hard to hit as though fenced in
by an oak hedge. While Little John rolled over and over
in silent joy.

Back and forth swayed the fighters, their cudgels
pounding this way and that, knocking off splinters and
bark, and threatening direst damage to bone and muscle
and skin. Back and forth they pranced kicking up a cloud
of dust and gasping for fresh air. From a little way off
you would have vowed that these two men were trying to
put out a fire, so thickly hung the cloud of battle over
them. Thrice did Robin smite the scarlet man—with such
blows that a less stout fellow must have bowled over.
Only twice did the scarlet man smite Robin, but the second blow was like to finish him. The first had been de-
livered over the knuckles, and though 'twas a glancing
stroke it well nigh broke Robin's fingers, so that he could
not easily raise his staff again. And while he was dancing
about in pain and muttering a dust-covered oath, the
other's staff came swinging through the cloud at one side—
zip!—and struck him under the arm. Down went Robin
as though he were a nine-pin—flat down into the dust of
the road. But despite the pain he was bounding up again
like an India-rubber man to renew the attack, when Little
John interfered.

"Hold!" said he, bursting out of the bushes and seizing
the stranger's weapon. "Hold, I say!"

"Nay," retorted the stranger quietly, "I was not offering
to smite him while he was down. But if there be a whole
nest of you hatching here by the waterside, cluck out the
other chicks and I'll make shift to fight them all."

"Not for all the deer in Sherwood!" cried Robin. "You are a good fellow and a gentleman. I'll fight no more with you, for verily I feel sore in wrist and body. Nor shall any of mine molest you henceforth."

Sooth to say, Robin did not look in good fighting trim. His clothes were coated with dirt, one of his hosen had slipped halfway down from his knee, the sleeve of his jerkin was split, and his face was streaked with sweat and dirt. Little John eyed him drolly.

"How now, good master," quoth he, "the sport you were to kick up has left you in sorry plight. Let me dust your coat for you."

"Marry, it has been dusted enough already," replied Robin; "and I now believe the Scripture saying that all men are but dust, for it has sifted me through and through and lined my gullet an inch deep. By your leave"—and he went to the brookside and drank deep and laved his face and hands.

All this while the stranger had been eyeing Robin attentively and listening to his voice as though striving to recall it.

"If I mistake not," he said slowly, at last, "you are the famous outlaw, Robin Hood of Barnesdale."

"You say right," replied Robin; "but my fame has been tumbling sadly about in the dust to-day."

"Now why did I not know you at once?" continued the stranger. "This battle need not have happened, for I came abroad to find you to-day, and thought to have remembered your face and speech. Know you not me, Rob, my lad? Hast ever been to Gamewell Lodge?"

"Ha! Will Gamewell, my dear old chum, Will Gamewell!" shouted Robin, throwing his arms about the other

in sheer affection. "What an ass I was not to recognize
you! But it has been years since we parted, and your
gentle schooling has polished you off mightily."

Will embraced his cousin no less heartily. "We are
quits on not knowing kinsmen," he said, "for you have
changed and strengthened much from the stripling with
whom I used to run foot races in old Sherwood."

"But why seek you me?" asked Robin. "You know I
am an outlaw and dangerous company. And how left
you mine uncle? and have you heard aught of late of—of
Maid Marian?"

"Your last question first," answered Will, laughing, "for
I perceive that it lies nearest your heart. I saw Maid
Marian not many weeks after the great shooting at Nottingham, when you won her the golden arrow. She prizes
the bauble among her dearest possessions, though it has
made her an enemy in the Sheriff's proud daughter. Maid
Marian bade me tell you, if I ever saw you, that she must
return to Queen Eleanor's court, but she could never forget the happy days in the greenwood. As for the old
Squire, he is still hale and hearty, though rheumatic withal.
He speaks of you as a sad young dog, but, for all that, is
secretly proud of your skill at the bow and of the way you
are pestering the Sheriff, whom he likes not. 'Tis for my
father's sake that I am now in the open, an outlaw like
yourself. He has had a steward, a surly fellow enough,
who, while I was away at school, boot-licked his way to
favor until he lorded it over the whole house. Then he
grew right saucy and impudent, but my father minded it
not, deeming the fellow indispensable in managing the
estate. But when I came back it irked me sorely to see the
fellow strut about as though he owned the place. He was
sly enough with me at first, and would brow-beat the

Squire only while I was out of earshot. It chanced one day, however, that I heard loud voices through an open window and paused to hearken. That vile servant called my father 'a meddling old fool.' 'Fool and meddler art thou thyself, varlet,' I shouted, springing through the window, '*that* for thy impudence!' and in my heat I smote him a blow mightier than I intended, for I have some strength in mine arm. The fellow rolled over and never breathed afterwards. I think I broke his neck or something the like. Then I knew that the Sheriff would use this as a pretext to hound my father, if I tarried. So I bade the Squire farewell and told him I would seek you in Sherwood."

"Now by my halidom!" said Robin Hood; "for a man 'scaping the law, you take it about as coolly as one could wish. To see you come tripping along decked out in all your gay plumage and trolling forth a roundelay, one would think you had not a care in all the world. Indeed I remarked to Little John here that I hoped your purse was not as light as your heart."

"Belike you meant *head*," laughed Will; "and is this Little John the Great? Shake hands with me, an you will, and promise me to cross a staff with me in friendly bout some day in the forest!"

"That will I!" quoth Little John heartily. "Here's my hand on it. What is your last name again, say you?"

" 'Tis to be changed," interposed Robin; "then shall the men armed with warrants go hang for all of us. Let me bethink myself. Ah!—I have it! In scarlet he came to us, and that shall be his name henceforth. Welcome to the greenwood, Will Scarlet!"

"Aye, welcome, Will Scarlet!" said Little John; and they all clasped hands again and swore to be true each to the other and to Robin Hood's men in Sherwood Forest.

VII

how Robin Hood Met Friar Tuck

The friar took Robin Hood on his back,
Deep water he did bestride,
And spake neither good word nor bad,
Till he came to the other side.

In summer time when leaves grow green, and flowers are fresh and gay, Robin Hood and his merry men were all disposed to play. Thus runs a quaint old ballad which begins the next adventure. Then some would leap and some would run and some try archery and some ply the quarter-staff and some fall to with the good broad sword. Some again would try a round at buffet and fisticuff; and thus by every variety of sport and exercise they perfected themselves in skill and made the band and its prowess well known throughout all England.

It had been a custom of Robin Hood's to pick out the best men in all the countryside. Whenever he heard of one more than usually skilled in any feat of arms he would seek the man and test him in personal encounter—which did not always end happily for Robin. And when he had found a man to his liking he offered him service with the bold fellows of Sherwood Forest.

Thus it came about that one day after a practice at

82

shooting, in which Little John struck down a hart at five hundred feet distance, Robin Hood was fain to boast.

"God's blessing on your heart!" he cried, clapping the burly fellow on the shoulder; "I would travel an hundred miles to find one who could match you!"

At this Will Scarlet laughed full roundly.

"There lives a curtal friar in Fountain's Abbey—Tuck, by name—who can beat both him and you," he said.

Robin pricked up his ears at this free speech.

"By our Lady," he said, "I'll neither eat nor drink till I see this same friar."

And with his usual impetuosity he at once set about arming himself for the adventure. On his head he placed a cap of steel. Underneath his Lincoln green he wore a coat of chain metal. Then with sword and buckler girded at his side he made a goodly show. But he also took with him his stout yew bow and a sheaf of chosen arrows.

So he set forth upon his way with blithe heart; for it was a day when the whole face of the earth seemed glad and rejoicing in pulsing life. Steadily he pressed forward by winding ways till he came to a green broad pasture land at whose edge flowed a stream dipping in and out among the willows and rushes on the banks. A pleasant stream it was, but it flowed calmly as though of some depth in the middle. Robin did not fancy getting his feet wet, or his fine suit of mail rusted, so he paused on the hither bank to rest and take his bearings.

As he sat down quietly under the shade of a drooping willow he heard snatches of a jovial song floating to him from the farther side; then came a sound of two men's voices arguing. One was upholding the merits of hasty pudding and the other stood out stoutly for meat pie, "especially"—quoth this one—"when flavored with young onions!"

"Gramercy!" muttered Robin to himself, "that is a tantalizing speech to a hungry man! But, odds boddikins! did ever two men talk more alike than those two fellows yonder!"

In truth Robin could well marvel at the speech, for the voices were curiously alike.

Presently the willows parted on the other bank, and Robin could hardly forbear laughing outright. His mystery was explained. It was not two men who had done all this singing and talking, but one—and that one a stout curtal friar who wore a long cloak over his portly frame, tied with a cord in the middle. On his head was a knight's helmet, and in his hand was a no more warlike weapon than a huge pasty pie, with which he sat down by the water's edge. His twofold argument was finished. The meat pie had triumphed; and no wonder! for it was the present witness, soon to give its own testimony.

But first the friar took off his helmet to cool his head, and a droll picture he made. His head was as round as an apple, and eke as smooth in spots. A fringe of close curling black hair grew round the base of his skull, but his crown was bare and shiny as an egg. His cheeks also were smooth and red and shiny; and his little gray eyes danced about with the funniest air imaginable. You would not have blamed Robin Hood for wanting to laugh, had you heard this serious two-faced talk and then seen this jovial one-faced man. Good humor and fat living stood out all over him; yet for all that he looked stout enough and able to take care of himself with any man. His short neck was thick like that of a Berkshire bull: his shoulders were set far back, and his arms sprouted therefrom like two oak limbs. As he sat him down, the cloak fell apart disclosing a sword and buckler as stout as Robin's own.

Nathless, Robin was not dismayed at sight of the weapons. Instead, his heart fell within him when he saw the meat pie which was now in fair way to be devoured before his very eyes; for the friar lost no time in thrusting one hand deep into the pie, while he crossed himself with the other.

Thereupon Robin seized his bow and fitted a shaft.

"Hey, friar!" he sang out, "carry me over the water, or else I cannot answer for your safety."

The other started at the unexpected greeting, and laid his hand upon his sword. Then he looked up and beheld Robin's arrow pointing full upon him.

"Put down your bow, fellow," he shouted back, "and I will bring you over the brook. 'Tis our duty in life to help each other, and your keen shaft shows me that you are a man worthy of some attention."

So the friar knight got him up gravely, though his eyes twinkled with a cunning light, and laid aside his beloved pie and his cloak and his sword and his buckler, and waded across the stream with waddling dignity. Then he took Robin Hood upon his back and spoke neither good word nor bad till he came to the other side.

Lightly leaped Robin off his back, and said, "I am much beholden to you, good father."

"Beholden, say you!" rejoined the other, drawing his sword; "then by my faith you shall e'en repay your score. Now mine own affairs, which are of a spiritual kind and much more important than yours which are carnal, lie on the other side of this stream. I see that you are a likely man and one, moreover, who would not refuse to serve the church. I must therefore pray of you that whatsoever I have done unto you, you will do also unto me. In short, my son, you must e'en carry me back again."

Courteously enough was this said; but so suddenly had the friar drawn his sword that Robin had no time to unsling his bow from his back, whither he had placed it to avoid getting it wet, or to unfasten his scabbard. So he was fain to temporize.

"Nay, good father, but I shall get my feet wet," he commenced.

"Are your feet any better than mine?" retorted the other. "I fear me now that I have already wetted myself so badly as to lay in a store of rheumatic pains by way of penance."

"I am not so strong as you," continued Robin; "that helmet and sword and buckler would be my undoing on the uncertain footing amidstream, to say nothing of your holy flesh and bones."

"Then I will lighten up, somewhat," replied the other calmly. "Promise to carry me across and I will lay aside my war gear."

"Agreed," said Robin; and the friar thereupon stripped himself; and Robin bent his stout back and took him up even as he had promised.

Now the stones at the bottom of the stream were round and slippery, and the current swept along strongly, waist-deep, in the middle. Moreover Robin had a heavier load than the other had borne, nor did he know the ford. So he went stumbling along now stepping into a deep hole, now stumbling over a boulder in a manner that threatened to unseat his rider or plunge them both clear under current. But the fat friar hung on and dug his heels into his steed's ribs in as gallant manner as if he were riding in a tourna-

ment; while as for poor Robin the sweat ran down him in torrents and he gasped like the winded horse he was. But at last he managed to stagger out on the bank and deposit his unwieldly load.

No sooner had he set the friar down than he seized his own sword.

"Now, holy friar," quoth he, panting and wiping the sweat from his brow, "what say the Scriptures that you quote so glibly?—Be not weary of well doing. You must carry me back again or I swear that I will make a cheese-cloth out of your jacket!"

The friar's gray eyes once more twinkled with a cunning gleam that boded no good to Robin; but his voice was as calm and courteous as ever.

"Your wits are keen, my son," he said; "and I see that the waters of the stream have not quenched your spirit. Once more will I bend my back to the oppressor and carry the weight of the haughty."

So Robin mounted again in high glee, and carried his sword in his hand, and went prepared to tarry upon the other side. But while he was bethinking himself what great words to use, when he should arrive thither, he felt himself slipping from the friar's broad back. He clutched frantically to save himself but had too round a surface to grasp, besides being hampered by his weapon. So down went he with a loud splash into the middle of the stream, where the crafty friar had conveyed him.

"There!" quoth the holy man; "choose you, choose you, my fine fellow, whether you will sink or swim!" And he gained his own bank without more ado, while Robin thrashed and spluttered about until he made shift to grasp a willow wand and thus haul himself ashore on the other side.

Then Robin's rage waxed furious, despite his wetting, and he took his bow and his arrows and let fly one shaft after another at the worthy friar. But they rattled harmlessly off his steel buckler, while he laughed and minded them no more than if they had been hail-stones.

"Shoot on, shoot on, good fellow," he sang out; "shoot as you have begun; if you shoot here a summer's day, your mark I will not shun!"

So Robin shot, and passing well, till all his arrows were gone, when from very rage he began to revile him.

"You bloody villain!" shouted he, "you psalm-singing hypocrite! You reviler of good hasty pudding! Come but within reach of my sword arm, and, friar or no friar, I'll shave your tonsure closer than ever bald-pated monk was shaven before!"

"Soft you and fair!" said the friar unconcernedly; "hard words are cheap, and you may need your wind presently. An you would like a bout with swords, meet me halfway i' the stream."

And with this speech the friar waded into the brook, sword in hand, where he was met half-way by the impetuous outlaw.

Thereupon began a fierce and mighty battle. Up and down, in and out, back and forth they fought. The swords flashed in the rays of the declining sun and then met with a clash that would have shivered less sturdy weapons or disarmed less sturdy wielders. Many a smart blow was landed, but each perceived that the other wore an undercoat of linked mail which might not be pierced. Nathless, their ribs ached at the force of the blows. Once and again they paused by mutual consent and caught breath and looked hard each at the other; for never had either met so stout a fellow.

Finally in a furious onset of lunge and parry Robin's foot stepped on a rolling stone, and he went down upon his knees. But his antagonist would not take this advantage: he paused until Robin should get upon his feet.

"Now by our Lady!" cried the outlaw, using his favorite oath, "you are the fairest swordsman that I have met in many a long day. I would beg a boon of you."

"What is it?" said the other.

"Give me leave to set my horn to my mouth and blow three blasts thereon."

"That will I do," said the curtal friar, "blow till your breath fails, an it please you."

Then—says the old ballad—Robin Hood set his horn to his mouth and blew three mighty blasts; and half a hundred yeomen, with bows bent, came raking over the lee.

"Whose men are these," said the friar, "that come so hastily?"

"These men are mine," said Robin Hood, feeling that his time to laugh was come at last.

Then said the friar in his turn, "A boon, a boon, the like

I gave to you. Give me leave to set my fist to my mouth and whistle three blasts thereon."

"That will I do," said Robin, "or else I were lacking in courtesy."

The friar set his fist to his mouth and put the horn to shame by the piercing whistles he blew; whereupon half a hundred great dogs came running and jumping so swiftly that they had reached their bank as soon as Robin Hood's men had reached his side.

Then followed a rare foolish conflict. Stutely, Much, Little John and the other outlaws, began sending their arrows whizzing toward the opposite bank; but the dogs, which were taught of the friar, dodged the missiles cleverly and ran and fetched them back again in their mouths, just as the dogs of to-day catch sticks.

"I have never seen the like of this in my days!" cried Little John, amazed. " 'Tis rank sorcery and witchcraft."

"Take off your dogs, Friar Tuck!" shouted Will Scarlet, who had but then run up, and who now stood laughing heartily at the scene.

"Friar Tuck!" exclaimed Robin, astounded. "Are you Friar Tuck? Then am I your friend, for you are he I came to seek."

"I am but a poor anchorite, a curtal friar," said the other, whistling to his pack, "by name Friar Tuck of Fountain's Dale. For seven years have I tended the Abbey here, preached o' Sundays, and married and christened and buried folk—aye and fought too, if need were; and if it smacks not too much of boasting, I have not yet met the knight or trooper or yeoman that I would yield before. But yours is a stout blade. I would fain know you."

" 'Tis Robin Hood, the outlaw, who has been assisting you at this christening," said Will Scarlet, glancing roguishly at the two opponents' dripping garments. And at this sally the whole band burst into a shout of laughter, in which Robin and Friar Tuck joined.

"Robin Hood!" cried the good friar presently, holding his sides; "are you indeed that famous yeoman? Then I like you well; and had I known you earlier, I would have both carried you across and shared my pasty pie with you."

"To speak soothly," replied Robin gaily, "'twas that same pie that led me to be rude. Now, therefore, bring it and your dogs and repair with us to the greenwood. We have need of you,—with this message came I to-day to seek you. We will build you a hermitage in Sherwood Forest, and you shall keep us from evil ways. Will you not join our band?"

"Marry, that will I!" cried Friar Tuck jovially. "Once more will I cross this much beforded stream, and go with you to the good greenwood!"

VIII

how Allan-a-Dale's Wooing Was Prospered

"What is thy name?" then said Robin
    Hood,
"Come tell me, without any fail,"
"By the faith o' my body," then said
    the young man,
"My name it is Allan-a-Dale."

FRIAR TUCK and Much the miller's son soon became right good friends over the steaming stew they jointly prepared for the merry men that evening. Tuck was mightily pleased when he found a man in the forest who could make pasties and who had cooked for no less person than the High Sheriff himself. While Much marveled at the friar's knowledge of herbs and simples and woodland things which savored a stew greatly. So they gabbled together like two old gossips and, between them, made such a tasty mess that Robin Hood and his stout followers were like never to leave off eating. And the friar said grace too, with great unction, over the food; and Robin said Amen! and that henceforth they were always to have mass of Sundays.

So Robin walked forth into the wood that evening with

94

his stomach full and his heart, therefore, in great contentment and love for other men. He did not stop the first
passer-by, as his manner often was, and desire a fight.

Instead, he stepped behind a tree, when he heard a man's
voice in song, and waited to behold the singer. Perhaps
he remembered, also, the merry chanting of Will Scarlet,
and how he had tried to give it pause a few days before.

Like Will, this fellow was clad in scarlet, though he did
not look quite as fine a gentleman. Nathless, he was a
sturdy yeoman of honest face and a voice far sweeter than
Will's. He seemed to be a strolling minstrel, for he bore a
harp in his hand, which he thrummed, while his lusty tenor
voice rang out with—

> "Hey down, and a down, and a down,
> I've a lassie back i' the town;
> Come day, come night,
> Come dark or light,
> She will wed me, back i' the town!"

Robin let the singer pass, caroling on his way.

" 'Tis not in me to disturb a light-hearted lover, this
night," he muttered, a memory of Marian coming back to
him. "Pray heaven she may be true to him and the wedding be a gay one 'back i' the town'!"

So Robin went back to his camp, where he told of the
minstrel.

"If any of ye set eyes on him after this," quoth he in
ending, "bring him to me, for I would have speech with
him."

The very next day his wish was gratified. Little John
and Much the miller's son were out together on a foraging
expedition when they espied the same young man; at
least, they thought it must be he, for he was clad in scarlet
and carried a harp in his hand. But now he came drooping along the way; his scarlet was all in tatters; and at
every step he fetched a sigh, "Alack and a well-a-day!"

Then stepped forth Little John and Much the miller's son.

"Ho! do not wet the earth with your weeping," said Little John, "else we shall all have lumbago."

No sooner did the young man catch sight of them than he bent his bow, and held an arrow back to his ear.

"Stand off! stand off!" he said, "what is your will with me?"

"Put by your weapon," said Much, "we will not harm you. But you must come before our master straight, under yon greenwood tree."

So the minstrel put by his bow and suffered himself to be led before Robin Hood.

"How now!" quoth Robin, when he beheld his sorry countenance, "are you not he whom I heard no longer ago than yesternight caroling so blithely about 'a lassie back i' the town'?"

"The same in body, good sir," replied the other sadly; "but my spirit is grieviously changed."

"Tell me your tale," said Robin courteously. "Belike I can help you."

"That can no man on earth, I fear," said the stranger; "nathless, I'll tell you the tale. Yesterday I stood pledged to a maid, and thought soon to wed her. But she has been taken from me and is to become an old knight's bride this very day; and as for me, I care not what ending comes to my days, or how soon, without her."

"Marry, come up!" said Robin; "how got the old knight so sudden vantage?"

"Look you, worship, 'tis this way. The Normans overrun us, and are in such great favor that none may say them nay. This old returned Crusader coveted the land whereon my lady dwells. The estate is not large, but all in her own right; whereupon her brother says she shall wed a title, and he and the old knight have fixed it up for to-day."

"Nay, but surely——" began Robin.

"Hear me out, worship," said the other. "Belike you think me a sorry dog not to make fight of this. But the old knight, look you, is not come-at-able. I threw one of his varlets into a thorn hedge, and another into a water-butt, and a third landed head-first into a ditch. But I couldn't do any fighting at all."

" 'Tis a pity!" quoth Little John gravely. He had been sitting cross-legged listening to this tale of woe. "What think you, Friar Tuck, doth not a bit of fighting ease a man's mind?"

"Blood-letting is ofttimes recommended of the leeches," replied Tuck.

"Does the maid love you?" asked Robin Hood.

"By our troth, she loved me right well," said the minstrel. "I have a little ring of hers by me which I have kept for seven long years."

"What is your name?" then said Robin Hood.

"By the faith of my body," replied the young man, "my name is Allan-a-Dale."

"What will you give me, Allan-a-Dale," said Robin Hood, "in ready gold or fee, to help you to your true love again, and deliver her back unto you?"

"I have no money, save only five shillings," quoth Allan; "but—are you not Robin Hood?"

Robin nodded.

"Then you, if any one, can aid me!" said Allan-a-Dale eagerly. "And if you give me back my love, I swear upon a book that I will be your true servant forever after."

"Where is this wedding to take place, and when?" asked Robin.

"At Plympton Church, scarce five miles from here; and at three o' the afternoon."

"Then to Plympton we will go!" cried Robin, suddenly springing into action; and he gave out orders like a general: "Will Stutely, do you have four-and-twenty good men over against Plympton Church 'gainst three o' the afternoon. Much, good fellow, do you cook up some porridge for this youth, for he must have a good round stomach—aye, and a better gear! Will Scarlet, you will see to decking him out bravely for the nonce. And Friar Tuck, hold yourself in readiness good book in hand, at the church. Mayhap you had best go ahead of us all."

The fat Bishop of Hereford was full of pomp and importance that day at Plympton Church. He was to celebrate the marriage of an old knight—a returned Crusader —and a landed young woman; and all the gentry thereabout were to grace the occasion with their presence. The church itself was gaily festooned with flowers for the ceremony, while out in the churchyard at one side brown ale flowed freely for all the servitors.

Already were the guests beginning to assemble, when the Bishop, back in the vestry, saw a minstrel clad in green walk up boldly to the door and peer within. It was Robin Hood, who had borrowed Allan's be-ribboned harp for the time.

"Now who are you, fellow?" quoth the Bishop, "and what do you here at the church-door with your harp and saucy air?"

"May it please your Reverence," returned Robin, bowing very humbly, "I am but a strolling harper, yet likened the best in the whole North Countree. And I had hope that my thrumming might add zest to the wedding to-day."

"What tune can you harp?" demanded the Bishop.

"I can harp a tune so merry that a forlorn lover will forget he is jilted," said Robin. "I can harp another tune that will make a bride forsake her lord at the altar. I can harp another tune that will bring loving souls together though they were up hill and down dale five good miles away from each other."

"Then welcome good minstrel," said the Bishop, "music pleases me right well, and if you can play up to your

prattle, 'twill indeed grace our ceremony.   Let us sample
your wares."

"Nay, I must not put finger to string until the bride and
groom have come.   Such a thing would ill fortune both
us and them."

"Have it as you will," said the Bishop, "but here comes
the party now."

Then up the lane to the church came the old knight,
preceded by ten archers liveried in scarlet and gold.   A

brave sight the archers made, but their master walked
slowly, leaning upon a cane and shaking as though in a
palsy.

And after them came a sweet lass leaning upon her
brother's arm. Her hair did shine like glistering gold, and
her eyes were like blue violets that peep out shyly at the
sun. The color came and went in her cheeks like the tint-
ing of a sea-shell, and her face was flushed as though she
had been weeping. But now she walked with a proud air,
as though she defied the world to crush her spirit. She had
but two maids with her, finikin lasses, with black eyes
and broad bosoms, who set off their lady's more delicate
beauty well. One held up the bride's gown from the
ground; the other carried flowers in plenty.

"Now by all the wedding bells that ever were rung!"
quoth Robin boldly, "this is the worst matched pair that
ever mine eyes beheld!"

"Silence, miscreant!" said a man who stood near.

The Bishop had hurriedly donned his gown and now
stood ready to meet the couple at the chancel.

But Robin paid no heed to him. He let the knight and
his ten archers pass by, then he strode up to the bride, and
placed himself on the other side from her brother.

"Courage, lady!" he whispered, "there is another minstrel near, who mayhap may play more to your liking."

The lady glanced at him with a frightened air, but read
such honesty and kindness in his glance that she brightened and gave him a grateful look.

"Stand aside, fool!" cried the brother wrathfully.

"Nay, but I am to bring good fortune to the bride by
accompanying her through the church-doors," said Robin,
laughing.

Thereupon he was allowed to walk by her side, unmolested, up to the chancel with the party.

"Now strike up your music, fellow!" ordered the Bishop.

"Right gladly will I," quoth Robin, "an you will let me choose my instrument. For sometimes I like the harp, and other times I think the horn makes the merriest music in all the world."

And he drew forth his bugle from underneath his green cloak and blew three winding notes that made the churchrafters ring again.

"Seize him!" yelled the Bishop; "there's mischief afoot! These are the tricks of Robin Hood!"

The ten liveried archers rushed forward from the rear of the church, where they had been stationed. But their rush was blocked by the onlookers who now rose from their pews in alarm and crowded the aisles. Meanwhile Robin had leaped lightly over the chancel rail and stationed himself in a nook by the altar.

"Stand where you are!" he shouted, drawing his bow, "the first man to pass the rail dies the death. And all ye who have come to witness a wedding stay in your seats. We shall e'en have one, since we are come into a church. But the bride shall choose her own swain!"

Then up rose another great commotion at the door, and four-and-twenty good bowmen came marching in with Will Stutely at their head. And they seized the ten liveried archers and the bride's scowling brother and the other men on guard and bound them prisoners.

Then in came Allan-a-Dale, decked out gayly, with Will Scarlet for best man. And they walked gravely down the aisle and stood over against the chancel.

"Before a maiden weds she chooses—an the laws of good

King Harry be just ones," said Robin. "Now, maiden,
before this wedding continues, whom will you have to
husband?"

The maiden answered not in words, but smiled with a
glad light in her eyes, and walked over to Allan and
clasped her arms about his neck.

"That is her true love," said Robin. "Young Allan instead of the gouty knight. And the true lovers shall be
married at this time before we depart away. Now my lord
Bishop, proceed with the ceremony!"

"Nay, that shall not be," protested the Bishop; "the bans
must be cried three times in the church. Such is the law
of our land."

"Come here, Little John," called Robin impatiently; and
he plucked off the Bishop's frock from his back and put it
on the yeoman.

Now the Bishop was short and fat, and Little John was
long and lean. And he clapped the Bishop's cap on the tall
fellow's head. The gown hung loosely over Little John's
shoulders and came only to his waist. He was a fine
comical sight, and the people began to laugh consumedly
at him. Howbeit the Bishop confronted him with speech-
less rage.

"By the faith o' my body," said Robin, "this cloth makes
you a fine man. You're the finest Bishop that ever I saw
in my life. Now cry the bans."

So Little John clambered awkwardly into the quire, his
short gown fluttering gayly; and he called the bans for the
marriage of the maid and Allan-a-Dale once, twice, and
thrice.

"That's not enough," said Robin; "your gown is so short
that you must talk longer."

Then Little John asked them in the church, four, five, six, and seven times.

"Good enough!" said Robin. "Now belike I see a worthy friar in the back of this church who can say a better service than ever my lord Bishop of Hereford. My lord Bishop shall be witness and seal the papers, but do you, good friar, bless this pair with book and candle."

So Friar Tuck, who all along has been back in one corner of the church, came forward; and Allan and his maid kneeled before him, while the old knight, held an unwilling witness, gnashed his teeth in impotent rage; and the friar began with the ceremony.

When he asked, "Who giveth this woman?" Robin stepped up and answered in a clear voice:

"I do! I, Robin Hood of Barnesdale and Sherwood! And he who takes her from Allan-a-Dale shall buy her full dearly."

So the twain were declared man and wife and duly blessed; and the bride was kissed by each sturdy yeoman beginning with Robin Hood.

Now I cannot end this jolly tale better than in the words of the ballad which came out of the happening and which has been sung in the villages and countryside ever since:

> And thus having end of this merry wedding,
>   The bride looked as fresh as a queen;
> And so they turned to the merry greenwood,
>   Amongst the leaves so green.

IX

how The Widow's
Three Sons
Were Rescued

Now Robin Hood is to Nottingham
  gone,
  With a link a down and a down,
And there he met with the proud
  Sheriff,
  Was walking along the town.

THE wedding-party was a merry one
that left Plympton Church, I ween; but not so merry were
the ones left behind. My lord Bishop of Hereford was
stuck up in the organ-loft and left, gownless and fuming.
The ten liveried archers were variously disposed about the
church to keep him company; two of them being locked
in a tiny crypt, three in the belfry, "to ring us a wedding
peal," as Robin said; and the others under quire seats or in
the vestry. The bride's brother at her entreaty was released, but bidden not to return to the church that day or
interfere with his sister again on pain of death. While the
rusty old knight was forced to climb a high tree, where he
sat insecurely perched among the branches, feebly cursing
the party as it departed.

106

It was then approaching sundown, but none of the retainers or villagers dared rescue the imprisoned ones that night, for fear of Robin Hood's men. So it was not until sunup the next day that they were released. The Bishop and the old knight, stiff as they were, did not delay longer than for breakfast, but—so great was their rage and shame—made straight to Nottingham and levied the Sheriff's forces. The Sheriff himself was not anxious to try conclusions again with Robin in the open. Perhaps he had some slight scruples regarding his oath. But the others swore that they would go straight to the King, if he did not help them, so he was fain to consent.

A force of an hundred picked men from the Royal Foresters and swordsmen of the shire was gathered together and marched straightway into the greenwood. There, as fortune would have it, they surprised some score of outlaws hunting, and instantly gave chase. But they could not surround the outlaws, who kept well in the lead, ever and anon dropping behind a log or boulder to speed back a shaft which meant mischief to the pursuers. One shaft indeed carried off the Sheriff's hat and caused that worthy man to fall forward upon his horse's neck from sheer terror; while five other arrows landed in the fleshy parts of Foresters' arms.

But the attacking party was not wholly unsuccessful. One outlaw in his flight stumbled and fell; when two others instantly stopped and helped to put him on his feet again. They were the widow's three sons, Stout Will, and Lester, and John. The pause was an unlucky one for them, as a party of Sheriff's men got above them and cut them off from their fellows. Swordsmen came up in the rear, and they were soon hemmed in on every side. But

they gave good account of themselves, and before they
had been overborne by force of numbers they had killed
two and disabled three more.

The infuriated attackers were almost on the point of
hewing the stout outlaws to pieces, when the Sheriff cried:
"Hold! Bind the villains! We will follow the law in
this and take them to the town jail. But I promise ye the
biggest public hanging that has been seen in this shire for
many changes of the moon!"

So they bound the widow's three sons and carried them
back speedily to Nottingham.

Now Robin Hood had not chanced to be near the scene
of the fight, or with his men; so for a time he heard nothing

of the happening. But that evening while returning to
camp he was met by the widow herself, who came weeping along the way.

"What news, what news, good woman?" said Robin
hastily but courteously; for he liked her well.

"God save ye, Master Robin!" said the dame wildly.
"God keep ye from the fate that has met my three sons!
The Sheriff has laid hands on them and they are con-
demned to die."

"Now, by our Lady! that cuts me to the heart! Stout
Will and Lester, and merry John! The earliest friends I
had in the band, and still among the bravest! It must not
be! When is this hanging set?"

"Middle the tinker tells me that it is for to-morrow noon," replied the dame.

"By the truth o' my body," quoth Robin, "you could not tell me in better time. The memory of the old days when you freely bade me sup and dine would spur me on, even if three of the bravest lads in all the shire were not imperiled. Trust to me, good woman!"

The old widow threw herself on the ground and embraced his knees.

" 'Tis dire danger I am asking ye to face," she said weeping; "and yet I knew your brave, true heart would answer me. Heaven help ye, good Master Robin, to answer a poor widow's prayers!"

Then Robin Hood sped straightway to the forest-camp, where he heard the details of the skirmish—how that his men had been out-numbered five to one, but got off safely, as they thought, until a count of their members had shown the loss of the widow's three sons.

"We must rescue them, my men!" quoth Robin, "even from out the shadow of the rope itself!"

Whereupon the band set to work to devise ways and means.

Robin walked apart a little way with his head leaned thoughtfully upon his breast—for he was sore troubled—when whom should he meet but an old begging palmer, one of a devout order which made pilgrimages and wandered from place to place supported by charity.

This old fellow walked boldly up to Robin and asked alms of him; since Robin had been wont to aid members of his order.

"What news, what news, thou foolish old man?" said Robin, "what news, I do thee pray?"

"Three squires in Nottingham town," quoth the palmer,

"are condemned to die. Belike that is greater news than the shire has had in some Sundays."

Then Robin's long-sought idea came to him like a flash.

"Come, change thine apparel with me, old man," he said, "and I'll give thee forty shillings in good silver to spend in beer or wine."

"O, thine apparel is good," the palmer protested, "and mine is ragged and torn. The holy church teaches that thou should'st ne'er laugh an old man to scorn."

"I am in simple earnest, I say. Come, change thine apparel with mine. Here are twenty pieces of good broad gold to feast thy brethren right royally."

So the palmer was persuaded; and Robin put on the old man's hat, which stood full high in the crown; and his cloak, patched with black and blue and red, like Joseph's coat of many colors in its old age; and his breeches, which had been sewed over with so many patterns that the original was scarce discernible; and his tattered hose; and his shoes, cobbled above and below. And while as he made the change in dress he made so many whimsical comments also about a man's pride and the dress that makes a man, that the palmer was like to choke with cackling laughter.

I warrant you, the two were comical sights when they parted company that day. Nathless, Robin's own mother would not have known him, had she been living.

The next morning the whole town of Nottingham was early astir, and as soon as the gates were open country-folk began to pour in; for a triple hanging was not held there every day in the week, and the bustle almost equaled a Fair day.

Robin Hood in his palmer's disguise was one of the first ones to enter the gates, and he strolled up and down and around the town as though he had never been there before in all his life. Presently he came to the market-place, and beheld thereon three gallows erected.

"Who are these builded for, my son?" asked he of a rough soldier standing by.

"For three of Robin Hood's men," answered the other. "And it were Robin himself, 'twould be thrice as high I warrant ye. But Robin is too smart to get within the Sheriff's clutches again."

The palmer crossed himself.

"They say that he is a bold fellow," he whined.

"Ha!" said the soldier, "he may be bold enough out behind stumps i' the forest, but the open market-place is another matter."

"Who is to hang these three poor wretches?" asked the palmer.

"That hath the Sheriff not decided. But here he comes now to answer his own questions." And the soldier came to stiff attention as the Sheriff and his body-guard stalked pompously up to inspect the gallows.

"O, Heaven save you, worshipful Sheriff!" said the palmer. "Heaven protect you! What will you give a silly old man to-day to be your hangman?"

"Who are you, fellow?" asked the Sheriff sharply.

"Naught save a poor old palmer. But I can shrive three souls and hang their bodies most devoutly."

"Very good," replied the other. "The fee to-day is thirteen pence; and I will add thereunto some suits of clothing for that ragged back of yours."

"God bless ye!" said the palmer. And he went with the soldier to the jail to prepare his three men for execution.

Just before the stroke of noon the doors of the prison opened and the procession of the condemned came forth.

Down through the long lines of packed people they walked to the market-place, the palmer in the lead, and the widow's three sons marching firmly erect between soldiers.

At the gallows foot they halted. The palmer whispered to them, as though offering last words of consolation; and the three men, with arms bound tightly behind their backs, ascended the scaffold, followed by their confessor.

Then Robin stepped to the edge of the scaffold, while the people grew still as death; for they desired to hear the last words uttered to the victims. But Robin's voice did not quaver forth weakly, as formerly, and his figure had stiffened bolt upright beneath the black robe that covered his rags.

"Hark ye, proud Sheriff!" he cried. "I was ne'er a hangman in all my life, nor do I now intend to begin that trade. Accurst be he who first set the fashion of hanging! I have but three more words to say. Listen to them!"

And forth from his robe he drew his horn and blew three loud blasts thereon. Then his keen hunting-knife flew forth and in a trice, Stout Will, Lester, and merry John were free men and had sprung forward and seized the halberds from the nearest soldiers guarding the gallows.

"Seize them! 'Tis Robin Hood!" screamed the Sheriff, "an hundred pounds if ye hold them, dead or alive!"

"I make it two hundred!" roared the fat Bishop.

But their voices were drowned in the uproar that ensued immediately after Robin blew his horn. He himself had drawn his sword and leaped down the stairs from the scaffold followed by his three men. The guard had closed around them in vain effort to disarm them, when "A rescue!" shouted Will Stutely's clear voice on one side of them, and "A rescue!" bellowed Little John's on the other;

and down through the terror-stricken crowd rushed four-score men in Lincoln green, their force seemingly twice that number in the confusion. With swords drawn they fell upon the guard from every side at once. There was a brief clash of hot weapons, then the guard scattered wildly, and Robin Hood's men formed in a compact mass around their leader and forced their way slowly down the market-place.

"Seize them! In the King's name!" shrieked the Sheriff. "Close the gates!"

In truth, the peril would have been even greater, had this last order been carried out. But Will Scarlet and Allan-a-Dale had foreseen that event, and had already overpowered the two warders. So the gates stood wide open, and toward them the band of outlaws headed.

The soldiers rallied a force of twice their number and tried resolutely to pierce their centre. But the retreating force turned thrice and sent such volleys of keen arrows from their good yew bows, that they kept a distance between the two forces.

And thus the gate was reached, and the long road leading up the hill, and at last the protecting greenwood itself. The soldiers dared come no farther. And the widow's three sons, I warrant you, supped more heartily that night than ever before in their whole lives.

X

how A Beggar Filled the Public Eye

Good Robin accost him in his way,
To see what he might be;
If any beggar had money,
He thought some part had he.

ONE bright morning, soon after the stirring events told in the last chapter, Robin wandered forth alone down the road to Barnesdale, to see if aught had come of the Sheriff's pursuit. But all was still and serene and peaceful. No one was in sight save a solitary beggar who came sturdily along his way in Robin's direction. The beggar caught sight of Robin, at the same moment, as he emerged from the trees, but gave no sign of having seen him. He neither slackened nor quickened his pace, but jogged forward merrily, whistling as he came, and beating time by punching holes in the dusty road with the stout pike-staff in his hand.

The curious look of the fellow arrested Robin's attention, and he decided to stop and talk with him. The fellow was bare-legged and bare-armed, and wore a long shift of a shirt, fastened with a belt. About his neck hung a stout, bulging bag, which was buckled by a good piece of leather thong.

116

He had three hats upon his head
  Together sticked fast;
He cared neither for the wind nor wet,
  In lands where'er he past.

The fellow looked so fat and hearty, and the wallet on his shoulder seemed so well filled, that Robin thought within himself, "Ha! this is a lucky beggar for me! If any of them have money, this is the chap, and, marry, he should share it with us poorer bodies."

So he flourished his own stick and planted himself in the traveler's path.

"Sirrah, fellow!" quoth he; "whither away so fast? Tarry, for I would have speech with ye!"

The beggar made as though he heard him not, and kept straight on with his faring.

"Tarry, I say, fellow!" said Robin again, "for there's a way to make folks obey!"

"Nay, 'tis not so," answered the beggar, speaking for the first time; "I obey no man in all England, not even the King himself. So let me pass on my way, for 'tis growing late, and I have still far to go before I can care for my stomach's good."

"Now, by my troth," said Robin, once more getting in front of the other, "I see well by your fat countenance, that you lack not for good food, while I go hungry. Therefore you must lend me of your means till we meet again, so that I may hie to the nearest tavern."

"I have no money to lend," said the beggar crossly. "Methinks you are as young a man as I, and as well able to earn a supper. So go your way, and I'll go mine. If you fast till you get aught out of me, you'll go hungry for the next twelvemonth."

"Not while I have a stout stick to thwack your saucy

bones!" cried Robin. "Stand and deliver, I say, or I'll dust
your shirt for you; and if that will not teach you manners,
then we'll see what a broad arrow can do with a beggar's
skin!"

The beggar smiled, and answered boast with boast.
"Come on with your staff, fellow! I care no more for it
than for a pudding stick. And as for your pretty bow—
that for it!"

And with amazing quickness, he swung his pike-staff
around and knocked Robin's bow clean out of his hand, so
that his fingers smarted with pain. Robin danced and
tried to bring his own staff into action; but the beggar
never gave him a chance. Biff! whack! came the pike-
staff, smiting him soundly and beating down his guard.

There were but two things to do; either stand there and
take a sound drubbing, or beat a hasty retreat. Robin
chose the latter—as you or I would probably have done—
and scurried back into the wood, blowing his horn as he
went.

"Fie, for shame, man!" jeered the bold beggar after him.
"What is your haste? We had but just begun. Stay and
take your money, else you will never be able to pay your
reckoning at the tavern!"

But Robin answered him never a word. He fled up hill
and down dale till he met three of his men who were
running up in answer to his summons.

"What is wrong?" they asked.

" 'Tis a saucy beggar," said Robin, catching his breath.
"He is back there on the highroad with the hardest stick
I've met in a good many days. He gave me no chance to
reason with him, the dirty scamp!"

The men—Much and two of the widow's sons—could
scarce conceal their mirth at the thought of Robin Hood

running from a beggar. Nathless, they kept grave faces, and asked their leader if he was hurt.

"Nay," he replied, "but I shall speedily feel better if you will fetch me that same beggar and let me have a fair chance at him."

So the three yeomen made haste and came out upon the highroad and followed after the beggar, who was going smoothly along his way again, as though he were at peace with all the world.

"The easiest way to settle this beggar," said Much, "is to surprise him. Let us cut through yon neck of woods and come upon him before he is aware."

The others agreed to this, and the three were soon close upon their prey.

"Now!" quoth Much; and the other two sprang quickly upon the beggar's back and wrested his pike-staff from his hand. At the same moment Much drew his dagger and flashed it before the fellow's breast.

"Yield you, my man!" cried he; "for a friend of ours awaits you in the wood, to teach you how to fight properly."

"Give me a fair chance," said the beggar valiantly, "and I'll fight you all at once."

But they would not listen to him. Instead, they turned him about and began to march him toward the forest. Seeing that it was useless to struggle, the beggar began to parley. "Good my masters," quoth he, "why use this violence? I will go with ye safe and quietly, if ye insist, but if ye will set me free I'll make it worth your while. I've a hundred pounds in my bag here. Let me go my way, and ye shall have all that's in the bag."

The three outlaws took council together at this.

"What say you?" asked Much of the others. "Our master will be more glad to see this beggar's wallet than his sorry face."

The other two agreed, and the little party came to a halt and loosed hold of the beggar.

"Count out your gold speedily, friend," said Much.

There was a brisk wind blowing, and the beggar turned about to face it, directly they had unhanded him.

"It shall be done, gossips," said he. "One of you lend me your cloak and we will spread it upon the ground and put the wealth upon it."

The cloak was handed him, and he placed his wallet upon it as though it were very heavy indeed. Then he crouched down and fumbled with the leather fastenings. The outlaws also bent over and watched the proceeding closely, lest he should hide some of the money on his person. Presently he got the bag unfastened and plunged his hands into it. Forth from it he drew—not shining gold —but handfuls of fine meal which he dashed into the eager faces of the men around him. The wind aided him in this, and soon there arose a blinding cloud which filled the eyes, noses, and mouths of the three outlaws till they could scarcely see or breathe.

While they gasped and choked and sputtered and felt around wildly for that rogue of a beggar, he finished the job by picking up the cloak by its corners and shaking it vigorously in the faces of his suffering victims. Then he seized a stick which lay conveniently near, and began to rain blows down upon their heads, shoulders, and sides, all the time dancing first on one leg, then on the other and crying, "Villains! rascals! here are the hundred pounds I promised. How do you like them? I' faith, you'll get all that's in the bag."

Whack! whack! whack! whack! went the stick, empha-

sizing each word. Howls of pain might have gone up
from the sufferers, but they had too much meal in their
throats for that. Their one thought was to flee, and they
stumbled off blindly down the road, the beggar following
them a little way to give them a few parting love-taps.

"Fare ye well, my masters," he said finally, turning the
other way; "and when next I come along the Barnesdale
road, I hope you will be able to tell gold from meal dust!"

With this he departed, an easy victor, and again went
whistling on his way, while the three outlaws rubbed the
meal out of their eyes and began to catch their breath
again.

As soon as they could look around them clearly they be-

held Robin Hood leaning against a tree trunk and survey-
ing them smilingly.   He had recovered his own spirits in
full measure, on seeing their plight.   "God save ye, gossips!" he said, "ye must, in sooth, have gone the wrong
way and been to the mill, from the looks of your clothes."

Then when they looked shamefaced and answered
never a word, he went on, in a soft voice,

"Did ye see aught of that bold begger, I sent you for,
lately?"

"In sooth, master," responded Much the miller's son,
"we heard more of him than we saw him.   He filled us so
full of meal that I shall sweat meal for a week.   I was born
in a mill and had the smell of meal in my nostrils from my

very birth, you might say, and yet never before did I see such a quantity of the stuff in so small space."

And he sneezed violently.

"How was that?" asked Robin demurely.

"Why we laid hold of the beggar, as you did order, when he offered to pay for his release out of the bag he carried upon his back."

"The same I coveted," quoth Robin as if to himself.

"So we agreed to this," went on Much, "and spread a cloak down, and he opened his bag and shook it thereon. Instantly a great cloud of meal filled the air, whereby we could neither see nor breathe; and in the midst of this cloud he vanished like a wizard."

"But not before he left certain black and blue spots to be remembered by, I see," commented Robin.

"He was in league with the evil one," said one of the widow's sons, rubbing himself ruefully.

Then Robin laughed outright, and sat him down upon the gnarled root of a tree, to finish his merriment.

"Four bold outlaws, put to rout by a sorry beggar!" cried he. "I can laugh at ye my men, for I am in the same boat with ye. But 'twould never do to have this tale get abroad —even in the greenwood—how that we could not hold our own with the odds in our favor. So let us have this little laugh all to ourselves, and no one else need be the wiser!"

The others saw the point of this, and felt better directly, despite their itching desire to get hold of the beggar again. And none of the four ever told of the adventure.

But the beggar must have boasted of it at the next tavern; or a little bird perched among the branches of a neighboring oak must have sung of it. For it got abroad, as such tales will, and was put into a right droll ballad which, I warrant you, the four outlaws liked not to hear.

XI

how Robin Hood Fought Guy of Gisborne

"I dwell by dale and down," quoth he,
"And Robin to take I'm sworn;
And when I am called by my right
name,
I am Guy of good Gisborne."

SOME weeks passed after the rescue
of the widow's three sons; weeks spent by the Sheriff in
the vain effort to entrap Robin Hood and his men. For
Robin's name and deeds had come to the King's ears, in
London town, and he sent word to the Sheriff to capture
the outlaw, under penalty of losing his office. So the Sheriff tried every manner of means to surprise Robin Hood in
the forest, but always without success. And he increased
the price put upon Robin's head, in the hope that the best
men of the kingdom could be induced to try their skill at
a capture.

Now there was a certain Guy of Gisborne, a hireling
knight of the King's army, who heard of Robin and of the
price upon his head. Sir Guy was one of the best men at
the bow and the sword in all the King's service. But his
heart was black and treacherous. He obtained the King's

leave forthwith to seek out the forester; and armed with the King's scroll he came before the Sheriff at Nottingham.

"I have come to capture Robin Hood," quoth he, "and mean to have him, dead or alive."

"Right gladly would I aid you," answered the Sheriff, "even if the King's seal were not sufficient warrant. How many men need you?"

"None," replied Sir Guy, "for I am convinced that forces of men can never come at the bold robber. I must needs go alone. But do you hold your men in readiness at Barnesdale, and when you hear a blast from this silver bugle, come quickly, for I shall have the sly Robin within my clutches."

"Very good," said the Sheriff. "Marry, it shall be done." And he sat about giving orders, while Guy of Gisborne sallied forth disguised.

Now as luck would have it, Will Scarlet and Little John and a half-score of others had gone to Barnesdale that very day with a woodsledge, to buy suits of Lincoln green for certain of the yeomen who had come out at the knees and elbows. But not deeming it best for all of them to run their necks into a noose, they parted just outside the town, and while John and the others tarried and watched on the outside, the other outlaw dashed quickly into the inn hard by the gates.

Presently whom should he see but this same Will flying madly forth from the gates again, closely pursued by the Sheriff and threescore men. Over the moat Will sprang, through the bushes and briars, across the swamp, over stocks and stones, up the woodland roads in long leaps like a scared jack rabbit. And after him puffed the Sheriff and his men, their force scattering out in the flight as one man would tumble head-first into a ditch, another mire up

in the swamp, another trip over a rolling stone, and still
others sit down on the roadside and gasp for wind like fish
out of water.

The other outlaws, seeing themselves outnumbered,
took to the woods and shelter. Little John, who was always a daredevil, lingered behind the rest. He could not
forbear laughing heartily at the scene, though he knew
that 'twould be anything but a laughing matter if Will
should stumble. And in truth one man was like to come
upon him. It was William-a-Trent, the best runner among
the Sheriff's men. He had come within twenty feet of
Scarlet and was leaping along with great bounds like a
greyhound, when John rose up quickly, drew his bow and
let fly one of his fatal shafts. It would have been better
for William-a-Trent to have been abed with sorrow—says
the ballad—than to be that day in the greenwood shade to
meet with Little John's arrow. He had run his last race.

The others halted a moment in consternation, when the
shaft came hurtling down from the hill; but looking up
they beheld none save Little John, and with a cry of fierce
joy they turned upon him. Meanwhile Will Scarlet had
reached the brow of the hill and sped down the other side.

"I'll just send one more little message of regret to the
Sheriff," said Little John, "before I join Will."

But this foolhardy deed was his undoing, for just as the
arrow left the string, the good yew bow that had never
before failed him snapped in twain.

"Woe worth, woe worth thee, wicked wood, that ere
thou grew on a tree!" cursed Little John, and planted his
feet resolutely in the earth, resolved to sell the path dearly;
for the soldiers were now so close upon him that he dared
not turn.

And a right good account of himself he gave that day,

dealing with each man as he came up according to his merit. And so winded were the pursuers when they reached the top of the hill that he laid out the first ten of them right and left with huge blows of his brawny fist.

But if six men can do more than three, a score can overcome one. A body of archers stood off at a prudent distance and covered Little John with their arrows.

"Now yield you!" panted the Sheriff. "Yield you, Little John or Reynold Greenleaf, or whatever else name you carry this day! Yield you, or some few of these shafts will reach your heart!"

"Marry, my heart has been touched by your words ere now," said Little John; "and I yield me."

So the Sheriff's men laid hold of Little John and bound

him fast with many cords, so fearful were they lest he should escape. And the Sheriff laughed aloud in glee, and thought of how he should avenge his stolen plate, and determined to make a good day's work of it.

"By the Saints!" he said, "you shall be drawn by dale and down, and hanged high on a hill in Barnesdale this very day."

"Hang and be hanged!" retorted the prisoner. "You may fail of your purpose if it be Heaven's will."

Back down the hill and across the moor went the company speedily, for they feared a rescue. And as they went the stragglers joined them. Here a man got up feebly out of the ditch and rubbed his pate and fell in like a chicken with the pip going for its dinner. Yonder came hobbling

a man with a lame ankle, or another with his shins torn by
the briars or another with his jacket all muddy from the
marsh. So in truth it was a tatterdemalion crew that
limped and straggled and wandered back into Barnesdale
that day. Yet all were merry, for the Sheriff had promised
them flagons of wine, and moreover they were to hang
speedily the boldest outlaw in England, next to Robin
Hood himself.

The gallows was quickly put up and a new rope provided.

"Now up with you!" commanded the Sheriff, "and let us
see if your greenwood tricks will avail you to-morrow."

"I would that I had bold Robin's horn," muttered poor
John; "methinks 'tis all up with me even as the Sheriff hath
spoken."

In good sooth the time was dire and pressing. The rope
was placed around the prisoner's neck and the men prepared to haul away.

"Are you ready?" called the Sheriff. "One—two——"

But before the "three" left his lips the faint sound of a
silver bugle came floating over the hill.

"By my troth, that is Sir Guy of Gisborne's horn," quoth
the Sheriff; "and he bade me not to delay answering its
summons. He has caught Robin Hood."

"Pardon, Excellency," said one of his men; "but if he has
caught Robin Hood, this is a merry day indeed. And let
us save this fellow and build another gallows and hang
them both together."

"That's a brave thought!" said the Sheriff, slapping his
knee. "Take the rascal down and bind him fast to the
gallows-tree against our return."

So Little John was made fast to the gallows-tree, while
the Sheriff and all his men who could march or hobble

went out to get Robin Hood and bring him in for the double hanging.

Let us leave talking of Little John and the Sheriff, and see what has become of Robin Hood.

In the first place, he and Little John had come near having a quarrel that self-same morning because both had seen a curious looking yeoman, and each wanted to challenge him singly. But Robin would not give way to his lieutenant, and that is why John, in a huff, had gone with Will to Barnesdale.

Meanwhile Robin approached the curious looking stranger. He seemed to be a three-legged creature at first sight, but on coming nearer you would have seen that 'twas really naught but a poorly clad man, who for a freak had covered up his rags with a capul-hide, nothing more nor less than the sun-dried skin of a horse, complete with head, tail, and mane. The skin of the head made a helmet; while the tail gave the curious three-legged appearance.

"Good-morrow, good fellow," said Robin cheerily, "methinks by the bow you bear in your hand that you should be a good archer."

"Indifferent good," said the other, returning his greeting; "but 'tis not of archery that I am thinking this morning, for I have lost my way and would fain find it again."

"By my faith, I could have believed 'twas your wits you'd lost!" thought Robin, smiling. Then aloud: "I'll lead you through the wood," quoth he, "an you will tell me your business. For belike your speech is much gentler than your attire."

"Who are you to ask me my business?" asked the other roughly.

"I am one of the King's Rangers," replied Robin, "set

here to guard his deer 'gainst curious looking strollers."

"Curious looking I may be," returned the other, "but no stroller. Hark ye, since you are a Ranger, I must e'en demand your service. I am on the King's business and seek an outlaw. Men call him Robin Hood. Are you one of his men?"—eyeing him keenly.

"Nay, God forbid!" said Robin; "but what want you with him?"

"That is another tale. But I'd rather meet with that proud outlaw than forty good pounds of the King's money."

Robin now saw how the land lay. "Come with me, good yeoman," said he, "and belike, a little later in the day, I can show you Robin's haunts when he is at home. Meanwhile let us have some pastime under the greenwood tree. Let us first try the mastery at shooting arrows."

The other agreed, and they cut down two willow wands of a summer's growth that grew beneath a brier, and set them up at a distance of threescore yards.

"Lead on, good fellow," quoth Robin. "The first shot to you."

"Nay, by my faith," said the other, "I will follow your lead."

So Robin stepped forth and bent his bow carelessly and sent his shaft whizzing toward the wand, missing it by a scant inch. He of the horse-hide followed with more care, yet was a good three-fingers' breadth away.

On the second round, the stranger led off and landed cleverly within the small garland at the top of the wand; but Robin shot far better and clave the wand itself, clean at the middle.

"A blessing on your heart!" shouted Capul-Hide; "never saw I such shooting as that! Belike you are better than

Robin Hood himself. But you have not yet told me your name."

"Nay, by my faith," quoth Robin, "I must keep it secret till you have told me your own."

"I do not disdain to tell it," said the other. "I dwell by dale and down, and to take bold Robin am I sworn. This would I tell him to his face, were he not so great a craven. When I am called by my right name, I am Guy of Gisborne."

This he said with a great show of pride, and he strutted back and forth forgetful that he had just been beaten at archery.

Robin eyed him quietly. "Methinks I have heard of you elsewhere. Do you not bring men to the gallows for a living?"

"Aye, but only outlaws such as Robin Hood."

"But pray what harm has Robin Hood done you?"

"He is a highway robber," said Sir Guy, evading the question.

"Has he ever taken from the rich that he did not give again to the poor? Does he not protect the women and children and side with the weak and helpless? Is not his greatest crime the shooting of a few King's deer?"

"Have done with your sophistry," said Sir Guy impatiently. "I am more than ever of opinion that you are one of Robin's men yourself."

"I have told you I am not," quoth Robin briefly. "But if I am to help you catch him, what is your plan?"

"Do you see this silver bugle?" said the other. "A long blast upon it will summon the Sheriff and all his men, when once I have Robin within my grasp. And if you show him to me, I'll give you the half of my forty pounds reward."

"I would not help hang a man for ten times forty pounds," said the outlaw. "Yet will I point out Robin to you for the reward I find at my sword's point. I myself am Robin Hood of Sherwood and Barnesdale."

"Then have at you!" cried the other, springing swiftly into action. His sword leaped forth from beneath the horse's hide with the speed born of long practice, and before Robin had come to guard, the other had smitten at him full and foul. Robin eluded the lunge and drew his own weapon.

"A scurvy trick!" quoth he grimly, "to strike at a man unprepared."

Then neither spoke more, but fell sternly to work—lunge and thrust and ward and parry—for two full hours the weapons smote together sullenly, and neither Robin Hood nor Sir Guy would yield an inch. I promise you that if you could have looked forth on the fight from behind the trunk of some friendly tree, you would have seen deadly sport such as few men beheld in Sherwood Forest. For the fighters glared sullenly at each other, the fires of hatred burning in their eyes. One was fighting for his life; the other for a reward and the King's favor.

Still circled the bright blades swiftly in the air—now gleaming in the peaceful sunlight—again hissing like maddened serpents. Neither had yet touched the other, until Robin, in an unlucky moment, stumbled over the projecting root of a tree; when Sir Guy, instead of giving him the chance to recover himself, as any courteous knight would have done, struck quickly at the falling man and wounded him in the left side.

"Ah, dear Lady in Heaven," gasped Robin, uttering his favorite prayer, "shield me now! 'Twas never a man's destiny to die before his day."

And adroitly he sprang up again, and came straight at
the other with an awkward but unexpected stroke. The
knight had raised his weapon high to give a final blow

when Robin reached beneath and across his guard. One swift lunge, and Sir Guy of Gisborne staggered backward with a deep groan, Robin's sword through his throat.

Robin looked at the slain man regretfully.

"You did bring it upon yourself," said he; "and traitor and hireling though you were, I would not willingly have killed you."

He looked to his own wound. It was not serious, and he soon staunched the blood and bound up the cut. Then he dragged the dead body into the bushes, and took off the horse's hide and put it upon himself. He placed his own cloak upon Sir Guy, and marked his face so none might tell who had been slain. Robin's own figure and face were not unlike the other's.

Pulling the capul-hide well over himself, so that the helmet hid most of his face, Robin seized the silver bugle and blew a long blast. It was the blast that saved the life of Little John, over in Barnesdale, for you and I have already seen how it caused the fond Sheriff to prick up his ears and stay the hanging, and go scurrying up over the hill and into the wood with his men in search of another victim. In five-and-twenty minutes up came running a score of the Sheriff's best archers.

"Did you signal us, lording?" they asked, approaching Robin.

"Aye," said he, going to meet the puffing Sheriff.

"What news, what news, Sir Guy?" said that officer.

"Robin Hood and Guy of Gisborne had a fight; and he that wears Robin's cloak lies under the covert yonder."

"The best news I have heard in all my life!" exclaimed the Sheriff, rubbing his hands. "I would that we could have saved him for the hanging—though I cannot now complain."

"The hanging?" repeated Robin.

"Yes. This is our lucky day on the calendar. After you left me we narrowly missed running one of the fellows—I believe 'twas Will Scarlet—to earth; and another who came to his relief we were just about to hang, when your horn blew."

"Who was the other?" asked the disguised outlaw.

"Whom do you suppose?" laughed the Sheriff.—"The best man in the greenwood, next to Robin Hood himself—Little John, Reynold Greenleaf!" For the Sheriff could not forget the name Little John had borne under his own roof at Nottingham.

"Little John!" thought Robin, with a start. Verily that was a lucky blast of the bugle!

"But I see you have not escaped without a scratch," continued the Sheriff, becoming talkative through pure glee. "Here, one of you men! Give Sir Guy of Gisborne your horse; while others of you bury that dog of an outlaw where he lies. And let us hasten back to Barnesdale and finish hanging the other."

So they put spurs to their horses, and as they rode Robin forced himself to talk merrily, while all the time he was planning the best way to succor Little John.

"A boon, Sheriff," he said, as they reached the gates of the town.

"What is it, worthy sir? You have but to speak."

"I do not want any of your gold, for I have had a brave fight. But now that I have slain the master, let me put an end to the man; so it shall be said that Guy of Gisborne dispatched the two greatest outlaws of England in one day."

"Have it as you will," said the Sheriff, "but you should have asked a knight's fee and double your reward, and it would have been yours. It isn't every man that can take Robin Hood."

"No, Excellency," answered Robin. "I say it without boasting, that no man took Robin Hood yesterday and none shall take him to-morrow."

Then he approached Little John, who was still tied to the gallows'-tree; and he said to the Sheriff's men, "Now stand you back here till I see if the prisoner has been shrived." And he stooped swiftly, and cut Little John's bonds, and thrust into his hands Sir Guy's bow and arrows, which he had been careful to take.

" 'Tis I, Robin!" he whispered. But, in truth, Little John knew it already, and had decided there was to be no hanging that day.

Then Robin blew three loud blasts upon his own horn, and drew forth his own bow; and before the astonished Sheriff and his men could come to arms the arrows were whistling in their midst in no uncertain fashion.

And look! through the gates and over the walls came pouring another flight of arrows! Will Scarlet and Will Stutely had watched and planned a rescue ever since the Sheriff and Robin rode back down the hill. Now in good time they came; and the Sheriff's demoralized force turned tail and ran, while Robin and Little John stood under the harmless gallows, and sped swift arrows after them, and laughed to see them go.

Then they joined their comrades and hasted back to the good greenwood, and there rested. They had got enough sport for one day.

XII

how Maid Marian
Came Back to
Sherwood Forest;
also, how Robin Hood
Came Before the Queen

> But Robin Hood, he himself had
>   disguis'd,
>   And Marian was strangely attir'd,
> That they proved foes, and so fell to
>   blows,
>   Whose valor bold Robin admir'd.
>
>   * *
>
> And when he came at London's court,
>   He fell down on his knee.
> "Thou art welcome, Lockesley," said
>   the Queen,
>   "And all thy good yeomandree."

Now it fell out that one day not long
thereafter, Robin was minded to try his skill at hunting.
And not knowing whom he might meet in his rambles, he
stained his face and put on a sorry-looking jacket and a
long cloak before he sallied forth. As he walked, the

139

peacefulness of the morning came upon him, and brought
back to his memory the early days so long ago when he had
roamed these same glades with Marian. How sweet they
seemed to him now, and how far away! Marian, too, the
dainty friend of his youth—would he ever see her again?
He had thought of her very often of late, and each time
with increasing desire to hear her clear voice and musical
laugh, and see her eyes light up at his coming.

Perhaps the happiness of Allan-a-Dale and his lady had
caused Robin's heart-strings to vibrate more strongly; perhaps, too, the coming of Will Scarlet. But, certes, Robin
was anything but a hunter this bright morning as he
walked along with head drooping in a most love-lorn way.

Presently a hart entered the glade in full view of him,
grazing peacefully, and instantly the man of action awoke.
His bow was drawn and a shaft all but loosed, when the
beast fell suddenly, pierced by a clever arrow from the
far side of the glade.

Then a handsome little page sprang gleefully from the
covert and ran toward the dying animal. This was
plainly the archer, for he flourished his bow aloft, and
likewise bore a sword at his side, though for all that he
looked a mere lad.

Robin approached the hart from the other side.

"How dare you shoot the King's beasts, stripling?" he
asked severely.

"I have as much right to shoot them as the King himself," answered the page haughtily. "How dare you
question me?"

The voice stirred Robin strongly. It seemed to chime
into his memories of the old days. He looked at the page
sharply and the other returned the glance, straight and
unafraid.

Louis Slobodkin

"Who are you, my lad?" Robin said, more civilly.

"No lad of yours, and my name's my own," retorted the other with spirit.

"Softly! Fair and softly, sweet page, or we of the forest will have to teach you manners!" said Robin.

"Not if *you* stand for the forest!" cried the page, whipping out his sword. "Come, draw, and defend yourself!"

He swung his blade valiantly; and Robin saw nothing for it but to draw likewise. The page thereupon engaged him quite fiercely, and Robin found that he had many pretty little tricks at fencing. Nathless, Robin contented himself with parrying, and was loth to exert all his superior strength upon the lad. So the fight lasted for above a quarter of an hour, at the end of which time the page was almost spent and the hot blood flushed his cheeks in a most charming manner.

The outlaw saw his distress, and to end the fight allowed himself to be pricked slightly on the wrist.

"Are you satisfied, fellow?" asked the page, wincing a little at sight of the blood.

"Aye, honestly," replied Robin; "and now perhaps you will grant me the honor of knowing to whom I owe this scratch?"

"I am Richard Partington, page to Her Majesty, the Queen," answered the lad, with dignity; and again the sound of his voice troubled Robin sorely.

"Why come you to the greenwood alone, Master Partington?"

The lad considered his answer while wiping his sword with a small lace kerchief. The action brought a dim confused memory to Robin. The lad finally looked him again in the eye.

"Forester, whether or not you be a King's man, know

that I seek one Robin Hood, an outlaw, to whom I bring
amnesty from the Queen. Can you tell me aught of him?"
And while awaiting his answer, he replaced the kerchief
in his shirt. As he did so, the gleam of a golden trophy
caught the outlaw's eye.

Robin started forward with a joyful cry.

"Ah! I know you now! By the sight of yon golden
arrow won at the Sheriff's tourney, you are she on whom I
bestowed it, and none other than Maid Marian!"

"You—are——?" gasped Marian, for it was she—"not
Robin!"

"Robin's self!" said he gayly; and forthwith, clad as he
was in rags, and stained of face, he clasped the dainty page
close to his breast, and she forsooth yielded right willingly.

"But Robin!" she exclaimed presently, "I knew you not,
and was rude, and wounded you!"

" 'Twas nothing," he replied laughingly, "so long as it
brought me you."

But she made more ado over the sore wrist than Robin
had received for all his former hurts put together. And
she bound it with the little kerchief, and said, "Now 'twill
get well!" and Robin was convinced she spoke the truth,
for he never felt better in all his life. The whole woods
seemed tinged with a roseate hue, since Marian had come
again.

But she, while happy also, was ill at ease; and Robin,
with a man's slow discernment, at last saw that it was because of her boy's attire. He thought bluntly that there
was naught to be ashamed of, yet smilingly handed her
his tattered long cloak, which she blushingly put on, and
forthwith recovered her spirits directly.

Then they began to talk of each other's varied fortunes,
and of the many things which had parted them; and so

much did they find to tell that the sun had begun to decline well into the afternoon before they realized how the hours sped.

"I am but a sorry host!" exclaimed Robin, springing to his feet. "I have not once invited you to my wild roof."

"And I am but a sorry page," replied Marian; "for I had clean forgot that I was Richard Partington, and really did bring you a message from the Queen!"

"Tell me on our way home, and there you shall be entrusted to Mistress Dale. While the first of my men we meet will I send back for your deer."

So she told him, as they walked back through the glade, how that the fame of his prowess had reached the Queen's ears, in London town. And her Majesty had said, "Fain would I see this bold yeoman, and behold his skill at the long-bow." And the Queen had promised him amnesty if he and four of his archers would repair to London against the next tournament the week following, there to shoot against King Henry's picked men, of whom the King was right vain. All this Marian told in detail, and added:

"When I heard Her Majesty say she desired to see you, I asked leave to go in search of you, saying I had known you once. And the Queen was right glad, and bade me go, and sent this gold ring to you from off her finger, in token of her faith."

Then Robin took the ring and bowed his head and kissed it loyally. "By this token will I go to London town," quoth he, "and ere I part with the Queen's pledge, may the hand that bears it be stricken off at the wrist!"

By this time they were come to the grove before the cave, and Robin presented Maid Marian to the band, who treated her with the greatest respect. Will Scarlet was especially delighted to greet again his old time friend, while Allan-a-Dale and his good wife bustled about to make her welcome in their tiny thatched cottage.

That evening after they had supped royally upon the very hart that Marian had slain, Allan sang sweet songs of Northern minstrelsy to the fair guest as she sat by Robin's side, the golden arrow gleaming in her dark hair. The others all joined in the chorus, from Will Scarlet's baritone to Friar Tuck's heavy bass. Even Little John essayed to sing, although looked at threateningly by Much the miller's son.

Then Robin bade Marian repeat her message from the Queen, which Marian did in a way befitting the dignity of her royal mistress. After which the yeomen gave three cheers for the Queen and three more for her page, and drank toasts to them both, rising to their feet.

"Ye have heard," quoth Robin, standing forth, "how that Her Majesty—whom God preserve!—wishes but four men to go with me. Wherefore, I choose Little John and Will Stutely, my two lieutenants, Will Scarlet, my cousin, and Allan-a-Dale, my minstrel. Mistress Dale, also, can go with her husband and be company for the Queen's page. We will depart with early morning, decked in our finest. So stir ye, my lads! and see that not only your tunics are fresh, but your swords bright and your bows and arrows fit. For we must be a credit to the Queen as well as to the good greenwood. You, Much, with Stout Will Lester, and John, the widow's son, shall have command of the band while we are away; and Friar Tuck shall preside over the needs of your souls and stomachs."

The orders were received with shouts of approval, and toasts all around were drunk again in nut-brown ale, ere the company dispersed to rest after making ready for the journey.

The next morning was as fine a summer's day as ever you want to see, and the green leaves of the forest made a pleasing background for the gay picture of the yeomen setting forth.   Says the old ballad—it was a seemly sight to see how Robin Hood himself had dressed, and all his yeomanry.   He clothed his men in Lincoln green, and himself in scarlet red, with hats of black and feathers white to bravely deck each head.   Nor were the two ladies behindhand, I ween, at the bedecking.

Thus the chosen party of seven sallied forth being accompanied to the edge of the wood by the whole band, who gave them a merry parting and Godspeed!

The journey to London town was made without incident.   The party proceeded boldly along the King's highroad, and no man met them who was disposed to say them nay.   Besides, the good Queen's warrant and ring would have answered for them, as indeed it did at the gates of London.   So on they sped and in due course came to the palace itself and awaited audience with the Queen.

Now the King had gone that day to Finsbury Field, where the tourney was soon to be held, in order to look over the lists and see some of his picked men whom he expected to win against all comers.   So much had he boasted of these men, that the Queen had secretly resolved to win a wager of him.   She had heard of the fame of Robin Hood and his yeomen, as Marian had said; and Marian on her part had been overjoyed to be able to add a word in their favor and to set out in search of them.

To-day the Queen sat in her private audience-room

chatting pleasantly with her ladies, when in came Mistress Marian Fitzwalter attired again as befitted her rank of lady-in waiting. She courtesied low to the Queen and awaited permission to speak.

"How now!" said the Queen, smiling; "is this my lady Marian, or the page, Richard Partington?"

"Both, an it please Your Majesty. Richard found the man you sought, while Marian brought him to you."

"Where is he?" asked the Queen eagerly.

"Awaiting your audience—he and four of his men, likewise a lady of whose wooing and wedding I can tell you a pretty story at another time."

"Have them admitted."

So Marian gave orders to a herald, and presently Robin Hood and his little party entered the room.

Now the Queen had half-expected the men to be rude and uncouth in appearance, because of their wild life in the forest; but she was delightfully disappointed. Indeed she started back in surprise and almost clapped her hands. For, sooth to say, the yeomen made a brave sight, and in all the court no more gallant men could be found. Marian felt her cheeks glow with pride, at sight of the half-hidden looks of admiration sent forth by the other ladies-in-waiting.

Robin had not forgot the gentle arts taught by his mother, and he wore his fine red velvet tunic and breeches with the grace of a courtier. We have seen, before, what a dandified gentleman Will Scarlet was; and Allan-a-Dale, the minstrel, was scarcely less goodly to look upon. While the giant Little John and broad-shouldered Will Stutely made up in stature what little they lacked in outward polish. Mistress Dale, on her part, looked even more charming, if possible, than on the momentous day when she went to Plympton Church to marry one man and found another.

Thus came the people of the greenwood before the Queen, in her own private audience-room. And Robin advanced and knelt down before her, and said:

"Here am I, Robin Hood,—I and my chosen men! At Your Majesty's bidding am I come, bearing the ring of amnesty which I will protect—as I would protect Your Majesty's honor—with my life!"

"Thou art welcome, Lockesley," said the Queen, smiling graciously. "Thou art come in good time, thou and all thy brave yeomanry."

Then Robin presented each of his men in turn, and each fell on his knee and was greeted with most kindly words.

And the Queen kissed fair Mistress Dale upon the cheek,
and bade her remain in the palace with her ladies while
she was in the city. And she made all the party be seated
to rest themselves after their long journey. Fine wines
were brought, and cake, and rich food for their refreshment. And as they ate and drank, the Queen told them
further of the tourney to be held at Finsbury Field, and of
how she desired them to wear her colors and shoot for her.
Meantime, she concluded, they were to lie by quietly and
be known of no man.

To do all this, Robin and his men pledged themselves
full heartily. Then at the Queen's request, they related to
her and her ladies some of their merry adventures; whereat
the listeners were vastly entertained, and laughed heartily.

Then Marian, who had heard of the wedding at Plympton Church, told it so drolly that tears stood in the Queen's eyes from merriment.

"My lord Bishop of Hereford!" she said. " 'Twas indeed a comical business for him! I shall keep that to twit his bones, I promise you! So this is our minstrel?" she added presently, turning to Allan-a-Dale. "Methinks I have already heard of him. Will he not harp awhile for us today?"

Allan bowed low, and took a harp which was brought to him, and he thrummed the strings and sang full sweetly the border songs of the North Countree. And the Queen and all her ladies listened in rapt silence till all the songs were ended.

XIII

how The Outlaws Shot in King Harry's Tourney

The King is into Finsbury Field
Marching in battle 'ray;
And after follows bold Robin Hood,
And all his yeomen gay.

THE morning of the great archery contest dawned fair and bright, bringing with it a fever of impatience to every citizen of London town, from the proudest courtier to the lowest kitchen wench. Aye, and all the surrounding country was early awake, too, and began to wend their way to Finsbury Field, a fine broad stretch of practice ground near Moorfields. Around three sides of the Field were erected tier upon tier of seats for the spectators, with the royal boxes and booths for the nobility and gentry in the centre. Down along one end were pitched gayly colored tents for the different bands of King's archers. There were ten of these bands, each containing a score of men headed by a captain of great renown; so to-day there were ten of the pavilions, each bearing aloft the Royal Arms and vari-colored pennants which fluttered lightly in the fresh morning breeze.

Each captain's flag was of a peculiar color and device.

First came the royal purple streamer of Tepus, own bow-bearer to the King, and esteemed the finest archer in all the land. Then came the yellow of Clifton of Bucking-hamshire; and the blue of Gilbert of the White Hand,—he who was renowned in Nottinghamshire; and the green of Elwyn the Welshman; and the white of Robert of Clou-desdale; and after them five other captains of bands, each a man of proved prowess. As the Queen had said afore-time, the King was mightily proud of his archers, and now held this tourney to show their skill and, mayhap, to recruit their forces.

The uprising tiers of seats filled early, upon this summer morning, and the merry chatter of the people went abroad like the hum of bees in a hive. The royal party had not yet put in an appearance, nor were any of the King's archers visible. So the crowd was content to hide its im-patience by laughing jibes passed from one section to another, and crying the colors of their favorite archers. In and out among the seats went hawkers, their arms laden with small pennants to correspond with the rival tents. Other vendors of pie and small cakes and cider also did a thrifty business, for so eager had some of the people been to get good seats, that they had rushed away from home without their breakfast.

Suddenly the gates at the far end, next the tents, opened wide, and a courier in scarlet and gold, mounted upon a white horse, rode in blowing lustily upon the trumpet at his lips; and behind him came six standard-bearers riding abreast. The populace arose with a mighty cheer. King Harry had entered the arena. He bestrode a fine white charger and was clad in a rich dark suit of slashed velvet with satin and gold facings. His hat bore a long curling ostrich plume of pure white, and he doffed it graciously

in answer to the shouts of the people. By his side rode the
Queen, looking regal and charming in her long brocade
riding-habit; while immediately behind them came Prince
Richard and Prince John, each attired in knightly coats of
mail and helmets. Lords and ladies of the realm followed;
and, finally, the ten companies of archers, whose progress
round the field was greeted with hardly less applause than
that given the King himself.

The King and Queen dismounted from their steeds,
ascended the steps of the royal box, and seated themselves
upon two thrones, decked with purple and gold trappings,
upon a dais sheltered by striped canvas. In the booths at
each side the members of the Court took their places;
while comely pages ran hither and thither bearing the
royal commands. 'Twas a lordly sight, I ween, this shift-
ing of proud courtiers, flashing of jeweled fans, and com-
mingly of bright colors with costly gems!

Now the herald arose to command peace, and soon the
clear note of his bugle rose above the roar of the crowd and
hushed it to silence. The tenscore archers ranged themselves in two long rows on each side of the lists—a gallant
array—while their captains, as a special mark of favor,
stood near the royal box.

"Come hither, Tepus," said the King to his bow-bearer.
"Come measure me out this line, how long our mark must
be."

"What is the reward?" then asked the Queen.

"That will the herald presently proclaim," answered the
King. "For the first prize we have offered a purse containing twoscore golden pounds; for second, a purse containing twoscore silver pennies; and for third, a silver
bugle, inlaid with gold. Moreover, if the King's companies keep these prizes, the winning companies shall

have, first, two tuns of Rhenish wine; second, two tuns of
English beer; and, third, five of the fattest harts that run
on Dallom Lea.   Methinks that is a princely wager,"
added King Harry laughingly.

Up spake bold Clifton, secure in the King's favor.
"Measure no marks for us, most sovereign liege," quoth
he; "for such largess as that, we'll shoot at the sun and
the moon."

" 'Twill not be so far as that," said the King.   "But get
a line of good length, Tepus, and set up the targets at tenscore paces."

Forthwith, Tepus bowed low, and set up ten targets,
each bearing the pennant of a different company, while
the herald stood forth again and proclaimed the rules and
prizes.   The entries were open to all comers.   Each man,
also, of the King's archers, should shoot three arrows at the
target bearing the colors of his band, until the best bow-
man in each band should be chosen.   These ten chosen
archers should then enter a contest for an open target—
three shots apiece—and here any other bowman whatsoever was asked to try his skill.   The result at the open
targets should decide the tourney.

Then all the people shouted again, in token that the
terms of the contest pleased them; and the archers waved
their bows aloft, and wheeled into position facing their
respective targets.

The shooting now began, upon all the targets at once,
and the multitude had so much ado to watch them, that
they forgot to shout.   Besides, silence was commanded
during the shooting.   Of all the fine shooting that morning, I have not now space to tell you.   The full score of
men shot three times at each target, and then three times
again to decide a tie.   For, more than once the arrow shot

by one man would be split wide open by his successor.
Every man's shaft bore his number to ease the counting;
and so close would they stick at the end of a round, that
the target looked like a big bristle hair-brush. Then must
the spectators relieve their tense spirits by great cheering;
while the King looked mightily proud of his skilled bowmen.

At last the company targets were decided, and Tepus, as
was expected, led the score, having made six exact centres
in succession. Gilbert of the White Hand followed with
five, and Clifton with four. Two other captains had
touched their centre four times, but not roundly. While
in the other companies it so chanced that the captains had
been out-shot by some of the men under them.

The winners then saluted the King and Queen, and
withdrew for a space to rest and renew their bow-strings
for the keenest contest of all; while the lists were cleared
and a new target—the open one—was set up at twelvescore
paces. At the bidding of the King, the herald announced
that the open target was to be shot at to decide the title
of the best archer in all England; and any man there present was privileged to try for it. But so keen had been the
previous shooting, that many yeomen who had come to
enter the lists now would not do so; and only a dozen men
stepped forth to give in their names.

"By my halidom!" said the King, "these must be hardy
men to pit themselves against my archers!"

"Think you that your ten chosen fellows are the best
bowmen in all England?" asked the Queen.

"Aye, and in all the world beside," answered the King;
"and thereunto I would stake five hundred pounds."

"I am minded to take your wager," said the Queen mus-
ingly, "and will e'en do so if you grant me a boon."

"What is it?" asked the King.

"If I produce five archers who can out-shoot your ten, will you grant my men full grace and amnesty?"

"Assuredly!" quoth the King, in right good humor. "Nathless, I tell you now, your wager is in jeopardy, for there never were such bowmen as Tepus and Clifton and Gilbert!"

"Hum!" said the Queen, puckering her brow, still as though lost in thought. "I must see if there be none present to aid me in my wager. Boy, call hither Sir Richard of the Lea and my lord Bishop of Hereford!"

The two summoned ones, who had been witnessing the sport, came forward.

"Sir Richard," said she, "thou are a full knight and good. Would'st advise me to meet a wager of the King's, that I can produce other archers as good as Tepus and Gilbert and Clifton?"

"Nay, Your Majesty," he said, bending his knee. "There be none present that can match them. Howbeit,"—he added, dropping his voice—"I have heard of some who lie hid in Sherwood Forest who could show them strange targets."

The Queen smiled and dismissed him.

"Come hither, my lord Bishop of Hereford," quoth she, "would'st thou advance a sum to support my wager 'gainst the King?"

"Nay, Your Majesty," said the fat Bishop, "an you pardon me, I'd not lay down a penny on such a bet. For by my silver mitre, the King's archers are men who have no peers."

"But suppose I found men whom *thou knewest* to be masters at the bow," she insisted roguishly, "would'st thou not back them? Belike, I have heard that there be men

round about Nottingham and Plympton who carry such matters with a high hand!"

The Bishop glanced nervously around, as if half expecting to see Robin Hood's men standing near; then turned to find the Queen looking at him with much amusement lurking in her eyes.

"Odds bodikins! The story of my misadventure must have preceded me!" he thought, ruefully. Aloud he said, resolved to face it out,

"Your Majesty, such tales are idle and exaggerated. An you pardon me, I would add to the King's wager that his men are invincible."

"As it pleases thee," replied the Queen imperturbably. "How much?"

"Here is my purse," said the Bishop uneasily. "It contains fifteen score nobles, or near an hundred pounds."

"I'll take it at even money," she said, dismissing him; "and Your Majesty"—turning to the King, who had been conversing with the two princes and certain of the nobles —"I accept your wager of five hundred pounds."

"Very good," said the King, laughing as though it were a great jest. "But what has minded you to take such interest in the sport, of a sudden?"

"It is as I have said. I have found five men whom I will pit against any you may produce."

"Then we will try their skill speedily," quoth the King. "How say you, if first we decide this open target and then match the five best thereat against your unknown champions?"

"Agreed," said the Queen. Thereupon she signed to Maid Marian to step forward, from a near-by booth where she sat with other ladies-in-waiting, and whispered something in her ear. Marian courtesied and withdrew.

Now the ten chosen archers from the King's bands came forth again and took their stand; and with them stood forth the twelve untried men from the open lists. Again the crowd was stilled, and every eye hung upon the speeding of the shafts. Slowly but skilfully each man shot, and as his shaft struck within the inner ring a deep breath broke from the multitude like the sound of the wind upon the seashore. And now Gilbert of the White Hand led the shooting, and 'twas only by the space of a hair's-breadth upon the line that Tepus tied his score. Stout Elwyn, the Welshman, took third place; one of the private archers, named Geoffrey, came fourth; while Clifton must needs content himself with fifth. The men from the open lists shot fairly true, but nervousness and fear of ridicule wrought their undoing.

The herald then came forward again, and, instead of announcing the prize-winners, proclaimed that there was to be a final contest. Two men had tied for first place, declared His Majesty the King, and three others were entitled to honors. Now all these five were to shoot again, and they were to be pitted against five others of the Queen's choosing—men who had not yet shot upon that day.

A thrill of astonishment and excitement swept around the arena. "Who were these men of the Queen's choosing?" was upon every lip. The hubbub of eager voices grew intense; and in the midst of it all, the gate at the far end of the field opened and five men entered and escorted a lady upon horseback across the arena to the royal box. The lady was instantly recognized as Mistress Marian of the Queen's household, but no one seemed to know the faces of her escort. Four were clad in Lincoln green, while the fifth, who seemed to be the leader, was dressed

in a brave suit of scarlet red. For arms, they carried
simply a stout bow, a sheaf of new arrows, and a short
hunting-knife.

When the little party came before the dais on which the
King and Queen sat, the yeomen doffed their caps humbly,
while Maid Marian was assisted to dismount.

"Your Gracious Majesty," she said, addressing the
Queen, "these be the men for whom you sent me, and who
are now come to wear your colors and serve you in the
tourney."

The Queen leaned forward and handed them each a
scarf of green and gold.

"Lockesley," she said, in a clear voice, "I thank thee and
thy men for this service. Know that I have laid a wager
with the King that ye can outshoot the best five whom he
has found in all his bowmen."

The five men pressed the scarfs to their lips in token of
fealty.

The King turned to the Queen inquiringly.

"Who are these men you have brought before us?"
asked he.

Up came the worthy Bishop of Hereford, growing red
and pale by turns.

"Your pardon, my liege lord!" cried he; "but I must de-
nounce these fellows as outlaws. Yon man in scarlet is
none other than Robin Hood himself. The others are Little
John and Will Stutely and Will Scarlet and Allan-a-Dale—
all famous in the North Countree for their deeds of violence."

"As my lord Bishop personally knows!" added the
Queen significantly.

The King's brows grew dark. The name of Robin Hood
was well known to him, as to every man there present.

He felt his muscles tightening into bands of steel. (Page 22)

"Is this true?" he demanded sternly.

"Aye, my lord," responded the Queen demurely. "But, bethink you—I have your royal promise of grace and amnesty."

"That will I keep," said the King, holding in check his ire by a mighty effort. "But, look you! Only forty days do I grant of respite. When this time has elapsed, let these bold outlaws look to their safety!"

Then turning to his five victorious archers, who had drawn near, he added, "Ye have heard, my men, how that I have a wager with the Queen upon your prowess. Now here be men of her choosing—certain free shafts of Sherwood and Barnesdale. Wherefore look well to it, Gilbert and Tepus and Geoffrey and Elwyn and Clifton! If ye outshoot these knaves, I will fill your caps with silver pennies—aye, and knight the man who stands first. But if ye lose, I give the prizes, for which ye have just striven, to Robin Hood and his men, according to my royal word."

"Robin Hood and his men!" the saying flew round the arena with the speed of wild-fire, and every neck craned forward to see the famous fellows who had dared to brave the King's anger, because of the Queen.

Another target was now set up, at the same distance as the last, and it was decided that the ten archers should shoot three arrows in turn. Gilbert and Robin tossed up a penny for the lead, and it fell to the King's men. So Clifton was bidden to shoot first. Forth he stood, planting his feet firmly, and wetting his fingers before plucking the string. For he was resolved to better his losing score of that day. And in truth he did so, for the shaft he loosed sped true, and landed on the black bull's-eye, though not in the exact centre. Again he shot, and again he hit the black, on the opposite rim. The third shaft swerved downward and came within the second ring, some two fingers' breadth away. Nathless, a general cry went up, as this was the best shooting Clifton had done that day.

Will Scarlet was chosen to follow him, and now took his place and carefully chose three round and full-feathered arrows.

"Careful, my sweet coz!" quoth Robin, in a low tone. "The knave has left wide space at the centre for all of your darts."

But Robin gave Will the wrong caution, for over-much care spoiled his aim. His first shaft flew wide and lodged in the second ring even further away than the worst shot of Clifton.

"Your pardon, coz!" quoth Robin hastily. "Bid care go to the bottom of the sea, and do you loose your string before it sticks to your fingers!"

And Will profited by this hint, and loosed his next two shafts as freely as though they flew along a Sherwood glade. Each struck upon the bull's-eye, and one even nearer the centre than his rival's mark. Yet the total score was adjudged in favor of Clifton. At this Will Scarlet bit his lip, but said no word, while the crowd shouted and waved yellow flags for very joy that the King's man had overcome the outlaw. They knew, also, that this demonstration would please the King.

The target was now cleared for the next two contestants —Geoffrey and Allan-a-Dale. Whereat, it was noticed that many ladies in the Queen's booths boldly flaunted Allan's colors, much to the honest pride which glowed in the cheeks of one who sat in their midst.

"In good truth," said more than one lady to Mistress Dale, "if thy husband can handle the longbow as skilfully as the harp, his rival has little show of winning!"

The saying augured well. Geoffrey had shot many good shafts that day; and indeed had risen from the ranks by virtue of them. But now each of his three shots, though well placed in triangular fashion around the rim of the bull's-eye, yet allowed an easy space for Allan to graze within. His shooting, moreover, was so prettily done, that he was right heartily applauded—the ladies and their gallants leading in the hand-clapping.

Now you must know that there had long been a friendly rivalry in Robin Hood's band as to who was the best shot, next after Robin himself. He and Will Stutely had lately decided their marksmanship, and Will had found that Robin's skill was now so great as to place the leader at the head of all good bowmen in the forest. But the second place lay between Little John and Stutely, and neither wished to yield to the other. So to-day they looked narrowly at their leader to see who should shoot third. Robin read their faces at a glance, and laughing merrily broke off two straws and held them out.

"The long straw goes next!" he decided, and it fell to Stutely.

Elwyn the Welshman was to precede him; and his score was no whit better than Geoffrey's. But Stutely failed to profit by it. His besetting sin at archery had even been an undue haste and carelessness. To-day these were increased by a certain moodiness, that Little John had outranked him. So his first two shafts flew swiftly, one after the other, to lodging places outside the Welshman's mark.

"Man! man!" cried Robin entreatingly, "you do forget the honor of the Queen, and the credit of Sherwood!"

"I ask your pardon, master!" quoth Will humbly enough, and loosing as he spoke his last shaft. It whistled

down the course unerringly and struck in the exact centre
—the best shot yet made.

Now some shouted for Stutely and some shouted for
Elwyn; but Elwyn's total mark was declared the better.
Whereupon the King turned to the Queen.

"What say you now?" quoth he in some triumph. "Two
out of the three first rounds have gone to my men. Your
outlaws will have to shoot better than that in order to save
your wager!"

The Queen smiled gently.

"Yea, my lord," she said. "But the twain who are left
are able to do the shooting. You forget that I still have
Little John and Robin Hood."

"And you forget, my lady, that I still have Tepus and
Gilbert."

So each turned again to the lists and awaited the next
rounds in silent eagerness. I ween that King Harry had
never watched the invasion of an enemy with more anxiety
than he now felt.

Tepus was chosen to go next, and he fell into the same
error with Will Scarlet. He held the string a moment too
long, and both his first and second arrows came to grief.
One of them, however, came within the black rim, and he
followed it up by placing his third in the full centre, just
as Stutely had done in his last. These two centres were
the fairest shots that had been made that day; and loud
was the applause which greeted this second one. But the
shouting was as nothing to the uproar which followed
Little John's shooting. That good-natured giant seemed
determined to outdo Tepus by a tiny margin in each sep-
arate shot; for the first and the second shafts grazed his
rival's on the inner side, while for the third Little John did
the old trick of the forest: he shot his own arrow in a grace-

ful curve which descended from above upon Tepus's final centre shaft with a glancing blow that drove the other out and left the outlaw's in its place.

The King could scarce believe his eyes. "By my halidom!" quoth he, "that fellow deserves either a dukedom or a hanging! He must be in league with Satan himself! Never saw I such shooting."

"The score is tied, my lord," said the Queen, "we have still to see Gilbert and Robin Hood."

Gilbert now took his stand and slowly shot his arrows, one after another, into the bull's eye. 'Twas the best shooting he had yet done, but there was still the smallest of spaces left—if you looked closely—at the very centre.

"Well done, Gilbert!" spoke up Robin Hood. "You are a foeman worthy of being shot against." He took his own place as he spoke. "Now if you had placed one of your shafts *there*"—loosing one of his own—"and another *there*" —out sped the second—"and another *there*"—the third was launched—"mayhap the King would have declared you the best bowman in all England!"

But the last part of his merry speech was drowned in the wild tumult of applause which followed his exploit. His first two shafts had packed themselves into the small space left at the bull's-eye; while his third had split down between them, taking half of each, and making all three appear from a distance as one immense arrow.

Up rose the King in amazement and anger.

"Gilbert is not yet beaten!" he cried. "Did he not shoot within the mark thrice? And that is allowed a best in all the rules of archery."

Robin bowed low.

"As it please Your Majesty!" quoth he. "But may I be allowed to place the mark for the second shooting?"

The King waved his hand sullenly. Thereupon Robin prepared another old trick of the greenwood, and got him a light, peeled willow wand which he set in the ground in place of the target.

"There, friend Gilbert," called he gayly; "belike you can hit that!"

"I can scarce see it from here," said Gilbert, "much less hit it. Nathless, for King's honor, I will try."

But this final shot proved his undoing, and his shaft flew harmlessly by the thin white streak. Then came Robin to his stand again, and picked his arrow with exceeding care, and tried his string. Amid a breathless pause he drew the good yew bow back to his ear, glanced along the shaft, and let the feathered missile fly. Straight it sped, singing a keen note of triumph as it went. The willow wand was split in twain, as though it had met a hunter's knife.

"Verily, I think your bow is armed with witchcraft!" cried Gilbert. "For I did not believe such shooting possible."

"You should come to see our merry lads in the greenwood," retorted Robin lightly. "For willow wands do not grow upon the cobblestones of London town."

Meanwhile the King, in great wrath, had risen to depart, first signing to the judges to distribute the prizes. Never a word said he, of good or ill, to the Queen, but mounted his horse and, followed by his sons and knights, rode off the field. The archers dropped upon one knee as he passed, but he gave them a single baleful look and was gone.

Then the Queen beckoned the outlaws to approach, and they did so and knelt at her feet.

"Right well have ye served me," she said, "and sorry am I that the King's anger is aroused thereby. But fear ye not. His word and grace hold true. As to these prizes ye have gained, I add others of mine own—the wagers I have won from His Majesty the King and from the lord Bishop of Hereford. Buy with some of these moneys the best swords ye can find in London, for all your band, and call them the swords of the Queen. And swear with them to protect all the poor and the helpless and the women-kind who come your way."

"We swear," said the five yeomen solemnly.

Then the Queen gave each of them her hand to kiss, and arose and departed with all her ladies. And after they were gone, the King's archers came crowding around Robin and his men, eager to get a glimpse of the fellows about whom they had heard so much. And back of them came a great crowd of the spectators pushing and jostling in their efforts to come nearer.

"Verily!" laughed Little John, "they must take us for a Merry Andrew show!"

Now the judges came up, and announced to each man his prize, according to the King's command. To Robin was given the purse containing twoscore golden pounds; to Little John the twoscore silver pennies; and to Allan-a-Dale the fine inlaid bugle, much to his delight, for he was skilled at blowing sweet tunes upon the horn hardly less than handling the harp strings. But when the Rhenish wine and English beer and harts of Dallom Lea were spoken of, Robin said:

"Nay, what need we of wine or beer, so far from the greenwood? And 'twould be like carrying coals to Newcastle, to drive those harts to Sherwood! Now Gilbert and

Tepus and their men have shot passing well. Wherefore, the meat and drink must go to them, an they will accept it of us."

"Right gladly," replied Gilbert, grasping his hand. "Ye are good men all, and we will toast you every one, in memory of the greatest day at archery that England has ever seen, or ever will see!"

Thus said all the King's archers, and the hand of good-fellowship was given amid much shouting and clapping on the shoulder-blades.

And so ended King Harry's tourney, whose story has been handed down from sire to son, even unto the present day.

XIV

how Robin Hood Was Sought of the Tinker

And while the tinker fell asleep,
Robin made haste away,
And left the tinker in the lurch,
For the great shot to pay.

KING HARRY was as good as his word. Robin Hood and his party were suffered to depart from London—the parting bringing keen sorrow to Marian—and for forty days no hand was raised against them. But at the end of that time, the royal word was sent to the worthy Sheriff at Nottingham that he must lay hold upon the outlaws without further delay, as he valued his office.

Indeed, the exploits of Robin and his band, ending with the great tourney in Finsbury Field, had made a mighty stir through all England, and many there were to laugh boldly at the Nottingham official for his failures to capture the outlaws.

The Sheriff thereupon planned three new expeditions into the greenwood, and was even brave enough to lead them, since he had fifteenscore men at his beck and call each time. But never the shadow of an outlaw did he see, for Robin's men lay close, and the Sheriff's men knew not how to come at their chief hiding-place in the cove before the cavern.

Now the Sheriff's daughter had hated Robin Hood bitterly in her heart ever since the day he refused to bestow upon her the golden arrow, and shamed her before all the company. His tricks, also, upon her father were not calculated to lessen her hatred, and so she sought about for means to aid the Sheriff in catching the enemy.

"There is no need to go against this man with force of arms," she said. "We must meet his tricks with other tricks of our own."

"Would that we could!" groaned the Sheriff. "The fellow is becoming a nightmare unto me."

"Let me plan a while," she replied. "Belike I can cook up some scheme for his undoing."

"Agreed," said the Sheriff, "and if anything comes of your planning, I will e'en give you an hundred silver pennies for a new gown, and a double reward to the man who catches the outlaw."

Now upon that same day, while the Sheriff's daughter was racking her brains for a scheme, there came to the Mansion House a strolling tinker named Middle, a great gossip and braggart. And as he pounded away upon some pots and pans in the scullery, he talked loudly about what *he* would do, if he once came within reach of that rascal Robin Hood.

"It might be that this simple fellow could do something through his very simplicity," mused the Sheriff's daughter, overhearing his prattle. "Odds bodikins! 'twill do no harm to try his service, while I bethink myself of some better plan."

And she called him to her, and looked him over—a big brawny fellow enough, with an honest look about his eye,

and a countenance so open that when he smiled his mouth
seemed the only country on the map.

"I am minded to try your skill at outlaw catching," she
said, "and will add goodly measure to the stated reward
if you succeed. Do you wish to make good your boasted
prowess?"

The tinker grinned broadly.

"Yes, your ladyship," he said.

"Then here is a warrant made out this morning by the
Sheriff himself. See that you keep it safely and use it to
good advantage."

And she dismissed him.

Middle departed from the house mightily pleased with
himself, and proud of his commission. He swung his crab-
tree staff recklessly in his glee—so recklessly that he imperiled the shins of more than one angry passer-by—and
vowed he'd crack the ribs of Robin Hood with it though he
were surrounded by every outlaw in the whole greenwood.

Spurred on by the thoughts of his own coming bravery,
he left the town and proceeded toward Barnesdale. The
day was hot and dusty and at noon-time he paused at a
wayside inn to refresh himself. He began by eating and
drinking and dozing, in turn, then sought to do all at once.

Mine host of the "Seven Does" stood by, discussing the
eternal Robin with a drover.

"Folk do say that my lord Sheriff has sent into Lincoln
for more men-at-arms and horses, and that when he has
these behind him, he'll soon rid the forest of these fellows."

"Of whom speak you?" asked the tinker, sitting up.

"Of Robin Hood and his men," said the host; "but go to
sleep again. You will never get the reward!"

"And why not?" asked the tinker, rising with great show
of dignity.

"Where our Sheriff has failed, and the stout Guy of Gisborne, and many more beside, it behooves not a mere tinker to succeed."

The tinker laid a heavy hand upon the inn-keeper's fat shoulder, and tried to look impressive.

"There is your reckoning, host, upon the table. I must e'en go upon my way, because I have more important business than to stand here gossiping with you. But be not surprised, if, the next time you see me, I shall have with me no less person than Robin Hood himself!"

And he strode loftily out the door and walked up the hot white road toward Barnesdale.

He had not gone above a quarter of a mile when he met a young man with curling brown hair and merry eyes. The young man carried his light cloak over his arm, because of the heat, and was unarmed save for a light sword at his side. The newcomer eyed the perspiring tinker in a friendly way, and seeing he was a stout fellow, accosted him.

"Good-day to you!" said he.

"Good-day to you!" said the tinker; "and a morrow less heating."

"Aye," laughed the other. "Whence come you? And know you the news?"

"What is the news?" said the gossipy tinker, pricking up his ear; "I am a tinker by trade, Middle by name, and come from over against Banbury."

"Why as for the news," laughed the stranger, "I hear that two tinkers were set i' the stocks for drinking too much ale and beer."

"If that be all your news," retorted Middle, "I can beat you clear to the end of the lane."

"What news have you? Seeing that you go from town

to town, I ween you can outdo a poor country yokel at
tidings."

"All I have to tell," said the other, "is that I am especially
commissioned"—he felt mightily proud of these big words
—"especially commissioned to seek a bold outlaw which
they call Robin Hood."

"So?" said the other, arching his brows. "How 'especially commissioned'?"

"I have a warrant from the Sheriff, sealed with the
King's own seal, to take him where I can; and if you can
tell me where he is, I will e'en make a man of you."

"Let me see the warrant," said the other, "to satisfy myself if it be right; and I will do the best I can to bring him
to you."

"That will I not," replied the tinker; "I will trust none
with it. And if you'll not help me to come at him I must
forsooth catch him by myself."

And he made his crab-tree staff whistle shrill circles in
the air.

The other smiled at the tinker's simplicity, and said:

"The middle of the road on a hot July day is not a good
place to talk things over. Now if you're the man for me
and I'm the man for you, let's go back to the inn, just beyond the bend of road, and quench our thirst and cool our
heads for thinking."

"Marry, come up!" quoth the tinker. "That will I! For
though I've just come from there, my thirst rises mightily
at the sound of your voice."

So back he turned with the stranger and proceeded to
the "Seven Does."

The landlord arched his eyebrows silently when he saw
the two come in, but served them willingly.

The tinker asked for wine, and Robin for ale. The wine

was not the most cooling drink in the cellars, nor the clear-
est headed. Nathless, the tinker asked for it, since it was
expensive and the other man had invited him to drink.
They lingered long over their cups, Master Middle emptying one after another while the stranger expounded at
great length on the best plans for coming at and capturing
Robin Hood.

In the end the tinker fell sound asleep while in the act
of trying to get a tankard to his lips. Then the stranger
deftly opened the snoring man's pouch, took out the warrant, read it, and put it in his own wallet. Calling mine
host to him, he winked at him with a half smile and told
him that the tinker would pay the whole score when he
awoke. Thus was Master Middle left in the lurch "for the
great shot to pay."

Nathless, the stranger seemed in no great hurry. He
had the whim to stay awhile and see what the droll tinker
might do when he awoke. So he hid behind a window
shutter, on the outside, and awaited events.

Presently the tinker came to himself with a prodigious
yawn, and reached at once for another drink.

"What were you saying, friend, about the best plan
(ya-a-a-ah!) for catching this fellow?—Hello!—where's
the man gone?"

He had looked around and saw no one with him at the
table.

"Host! host!" he shouted, "where is that fellow who was
to pay my reckoning?"

"I know not," answered the landlord sharply. "Mayhap he left the money in your purse."

"No he didn't!" roared Middle, looking therein. "Help!
help! I've been robbed! Look you, host, you are liable
to arrest for high treason! I am here upon the King's busi-

ness, as I told you earlier in the day. And yet while I did rest under your roof, thinking you were an honest man (hic!) and one loving of the King, my pouch has been opened and many matters of state taken from it."

"Cease your bellowing!" said the landlord. "What did you lose?"

"Oh, many weighty matters, I do assure you. I had with me, item, a warrant, granted under the hand of my lord High Sheriff of Nottingham, and sealed with the

King's own seal for the capture (hic!)—and arrest—and
overcoming of a notorious rascal, one Robin Hood of
Barnesdale. Item, one crust of bread. Item, one lump
(hic!) of solder. Item, three pieces of twine. Item, six
single keys (hic!), useful withal. Item, twelve silver pennies, the which I earned this week (hic!) in fair labor.
Item——"

"Have done with your items!" said the host. "And I
marvel greatly to hear you speak in such fashion of your

friend, Robin Hood of Barnesdale.   For was he not with you just now? and did he not drink with you in all good-fellowship?"

"Wh-a-at?   *That* Robin Hood?" gasped Middle with staring eyes.   "Why did you not tell me?"

"Faith, *I* saw no need o' telling you.   Did you not tell me the first time you were here to-day, that I need not be surprised if you came back with no less person than Robin Hood himself?"

"Jesu give me pardon!" moaned the tinker.   "I see it all now.   He got me to drinking, and then took my warrant, and my pennies, and my crust——"

"Yes, yes," interrupted the host.   "I know all about that. But pay me the score for both of you."

"But I have no money, gossip.   Let me go after that vile bag-o'-bones, and I'll soon get it out of him."

"Not so," replied the other.   "If I waited for you to collect from Robin Hood, I would soon close up shop."

"What is the account?" asked Middle.

"Ten shillings, just."

"Then take here my working-bag and my good hammer too; and if I light upon that knave, I will soon come back after them."

"Give me your leathern coat as well," said mine host; "the hammer and bag of tools are as naught to me."

"Gramercy!" cried Master Middle, losing what was left of his temper.   "It seems that I have escaped one thief only to fall into the hands of another.   If you will but walk with me out into the middle of the road, I'll give you such a crack as shall drive some honesty into your thick skull."

"You are wasting your breath and my time," retorted

the landlord. "Give me your things, and get you gone after your man, speedily."

Middle thought this to be good advice; so he strode forth from the "Seven Docs" in a black mood.

Ere he had gone half a mile, he saw Robin Hood walking demurely among the trees a little in front of him.

"Ho, there, you villain!" roared the tinker. "Stay your steps! I am desperately in need of you this day!"

Robin turned about with a surprised face.

"What knave is this?" he asked gently, "who comes shouting after me?"

"No knave! no knave at all!" panted the other, rushing up. "But an honest—man—who would have—that warrant —and the money for drink!"

"Why, as I live, it is our honest tinker who was seeking Robin Hood! Did you find him, gossip?"

"Marry, that did I! and I'm now going to pay him my respects!"

And he plunged at him, making a sweeping stroke with his crab-tree cudgel.

Robin tried to draw his sword, but could not do it for a moment through dodging the other's furious blows. When he did get it in hand, the tinker had reached him thrice with resounding thwacks. Then the tables were turned, for he dashed in right manfully with his shining blade and made the tinker give back again.

The greenwood rang with the noise of the fray. 'Twas steel against wood, and they made a terrible clattering when they came together. Robin thought at first that he could hack the cudgel to pieces, for his blade was one of Toledo—finely tempered steel which the Queen had given him. But the crab-tree staff had been fired and hardened and seasoned by the tinker's arts until it was like a bar of iron—no pleasant neighbor for one's ribs.

Robin presently found this out to his sorrow. The long reach and long stick got to him when 'twas impossible for him to touch his antagonist. So his sides began to ache sorely.

"Hold your hand, tinker," he said at length. "I cry a boon of you."

"Before I do it," said the tinker, "I'd hang you on this tree."

But even as he spoke, Robin found the moment's grace for which he longed; and immediately grasped his horn and blew the three well-known blasts of the greenwood.

"A murrain seize you!" roared the tinker, commencing afresh. "Up to your old tricks again, are you? Well, I'll have time to finish my job, if I hurry."

But Robin was quite able to hold his own at a pinch, and they had not exchanged many lunges and passes when up came Little John and Will Scarlet and a score of yeomen at their heels. Middle was seized without ceremony, while Robin sat himself down to breathe.

"What is the matter?" quoth Little John, "that you need sit so weariedly upon the highway side?"

"Faith, that rascally tinker yonder has paid his score well upon my hide," answered Robin ruefully.

"That tinker, then," said Little John, "must be itching for more work. Fain would I try if he can do as much for me."

"Or me," said Will Scarlet, who like Little John was always willing to swing a cudgel.

"Nay," laughed Robin. "Belike I could have done better, an he had given me time to pull a young tree up by the roots. But I hated to spoil the Queen's blade upon his tough stick or no less tough hide. Besides, he had a good quarrel with me. He had a warrant for my arrest which I stole from him."

"Also, item, twelve silver pennies," interposed the tinker, unsubdued; "item, one crust of bread, 'gainst my supper. Item, one lump of solder. Item, three pieces of twine. Item, six single keys. Item——"

"Yes, I know," quoth the merry Robin; "I stood outside the landlord's window and heard you count over your losses. Here they are again; and the twelve silver pennies are turned by magic into gold. Here also, if you will, is my hand."

"I take it heartily, with the pence!" cried Middle. "By my leathern coat and tools, which I shall presently have out of that sly host, I swear that I never yet met a man I liked as well as you! An you and your men here will take me, I swear I'll serve you honestly. Do you want a tinker? Nay, but verily you must! Who else can mend and grind your swords and patch your pannikins—and fight, too, when occasion serve? Mend your pots! mend your pa-a-ans!"

And he ended his speech with the sonorous cry of his craft.

By this time the whole band was laughing uproariously at the tinker's talk.

"What say you, fellows?" asked Robin. "Would not this tinker be a good recruit?"

"That he would!" answered Will Scarlet, clapping the new man on the back. "He will keep Friar Tuck and Much the miller's son from having the blues."

So amid great merriment and right good fellowship the outlaws shook Middle by the hand, and he took oath of fealty, and thought no more of the Sheriff's daughter.

We have already given many of the words of the old ballad which tells of this adventure. It is a rollicking song of a rollicking deed, and ends with Robin's speech after the jolly tinker was sworn into the fellowship:

> "In manhood he's a mettled man
>   And a metal-man by trade;
> Never thought I that any man
>   Should have made me so afraid.

> "And if he will be one of us,
>   We will take all one fare;
> And whatsoever we do get,
>   He shall have his rightful share."

> So the tinker was content
>   With them to go along,
> And with them a part to take:
>   And so I end my song.

XV

how **Robin Hood Was Tanned of the Tanner**

In Nottingham there lived a jolly tan-
ner,
*With a hey down, down, a down
down!*
His name was Arthur-a-Bland;
There was ne'er a squire in Notting-
hamshire
Dare bid bold Arthur stand.

And as he went forth, in a summer's
morning,
*With a hey down, down, a down
down!*
To the forest of merrie Sherwood,
To view the red deer, that range here
and there,
There met he with bold Robin
Hood.

THE Sheriff's daughter bided for
several days in the faint hope that she might hear tidings of
the prattling tinker. But never a word heard she, and she
was forced to the conclusion that her messenger had not

183

so much as laid eyes upon the outlaw. Little recked she
that he was, even then, grinding sword-points and sharp-
ening arrows out in the good greenwood, while whistling
blithely or chatting merrily with the good Friar Tuck.

Then she bethought herself of another good man, one
Arthur-a-Bland, a tanner who dwelt in Nottingham town
and was far-famed in the tourneys round about. He had
done some pretty tricks at archery, but was strongest at
wrestling and the quarter-staff. For three years he had
cast all comers to the earth in wrestling until the famous
Eric o' Lincoln broke a rib for him in a mighty tussle.
Howsoever, at quarter-staff he had never yet met his
match; so that there was never a squire in Nottinghamshire dare bid bold Arthur stand.

> With a long pike-staff on his shoulder,
>   So well he could clear his way
> That by two and three he made men flee
>   And none of them could stay.

Thus at least runs the old song which tells of his might.

"This is just the man for me!" thought the Sheriff's
daughter to herself; and she forthwith summoned him to
to the Mansion House and commissioned him to seek out
Robin Hood.

The warrant was quite to Arthur's liking, for he was
happiest when out in the forest taking a sly peep at the
King's deer; and now he reckoned that he could look at
them boldly, instead of by the rays of the moon. He could
say to any King's Forester who made bold to stop him: "I
am here on the King's business!"

"Gramercy! No more oak-bark and ditch-water and
the smell of half-tanned hides to-day!" quoth he, gaily.
"I shall e'en see what the free air of heaven tastes like,
when it sweeps through the open wood."

So the tanner departed joyfully upon his errand, but much more interested in the dun deer of the forest than in any two-legged rovers therein. This interest had, in fact, caused the Foresters to keep a shrewd eye upon him in the past, for his tannery was apt to have plenty of meat in it that was more like venison than the law allowed. As for the outlaws, Arthur bore them no ill-will; indeed he had felt a secret envy in his heart at their free life; but he was not afraid to meet any two men who might come against him. Nathless, the Sheriff's daughter did not choose a very good messenger, as you shall presently see.

Away sped the tanner, a piece of bread and some wine in his wallet, a good longbow and arrows slung across his shoulder, his stout quarter-staff in his hand, and on his head a cap of trebled raw-hide so tough that it would turn the edge of a broadsword. He lost no time in getting out of the hot sun and into the welcome shade of the forest, where he stalked cautiously about seeking some sign of the dun deer.

Now it so chanced that upon that very morning Robin Hood had sent Little John to a neighboring village to buy some cloth of Lincoln green for new suits for all the band. Some of the money recently won of the King was being spent in this fashion, 'gainst the approach of winter. Will Scarlet had been sent on a similar errand to Barnesdale some time before, if you remember, only to be chased up the hill without his purchase. So to-day Little John was chosen, and for sweet company's seek Robin went with him a part of the way until they came to the "Seven Does," the inn where Robin had recently played his prank upon Middle the tinker. Here they drank a glass of ale to refresh themselves withal, and for good luck; and Robin tarried a bit while Little John went on his errand.

Presently Robin entered the edge of the wood, when whom should he see but Arthur-a-Bland, busily creeping after a graceful deer that browsed alone down the glade.

"Now by Saint George and the Dragon!" quoth Robin to himself. "I much fear that yon same fellow is a rascally poacher come after our own and the King's meat!"

For you must know, by a curious process of reasoning, Robin and his men had hunted in the royal preserves so long that they had come to consider themselves joint owners to every animal which roamed therein.

"Nay!" he added, "this must be looked into! That cow-skin cap in sooth must hide a scurvy varlet!"

And forthwith he crept behind a tree, and thence to another, stalking our friend Arthur as busily as Arthur was stalking the deer.

This went on for quite a space, until the tanner began to come upon the deer and to draw his bow in order to tickle the victim's ribs with a cloth-yard shaft. But just at this moment Robin unluckily trod upon a twig which snapped and caused the tanner to turn suddenly.

Robin saw that he was discovered, so he determined to put a bold face on the matter, and went forward with some smart show of authority.

"Hold!" he cried; "stay your hand! Why, who are you, bold fellow, to range so boldly here? In sooth, to be brief, ye look like a thief that has come to steal the King's deer."

"Marry, it is scant concern of yours, what I look like!" retorted Arthur-a-Bland. "Who are you, who speak so bravely?"

"You shall soon find out who I am!" quoth Robin, determining to find some sport in the matter. "I am a keeper of this forest. The King knows that I am looking after his deer for him; and therefore we must stay you."

"Have you any assistants, friend?" asked the tanner calmly. "For it is not one man alone who can stop me."

"Nay truly, gossip," replied Robin. "I have a good yew bow, also a right sharp blade at my side. Nathless, I need no better assistant than a good oak-graff like unto yours. Give me a baker's dozen of minutes with it and it shall pleasure me to crack that pate of yours for your sauciness!"

"Softly, my man! Fair and softly! Big words never killed so much as a mouse—least of all yon deer which has got away while you were filling all the woods with your noisy breath. So choose your own playthings. For your sword and your bow I care not a straw; nor for all your arrows to boot. If I get but a knock at you, 'twill be as much as you'll need."

"Now by our Lady! Will you listen to the braggart?" cried Robin in a fine rage. "Marry, but I'll teach ye to be more mannerly!"

So saying he unbuckled his belt; and, flinging his bow upon the ground he seized hold of a young sapling that was growing near by. His hunting-knife soon had it severed and lopped into shape.

"Now come on, fellow!" said Arthur-a-Bland, seeing that he was ready. "And if I do not tan your hide for you in better shape than ever calfskin was turned into top-boots, may a murrain seize me!"

"Stay," said Robin, "methinks my cudgel is half a foot longer than yours. I would have them of even length before you begin your tanning."

"I pass not for length," bold Arthur replied; "My staff

is long enough, as you will shortly find out. Eight foot
and a half, and 'twill knock down a calf"—here he
made it whistle in the air—"and I hope it will knock down
you."

Forthwith the two men spat on their hands, laid firm
hold upon their cudgels and began slowly circling round
each other, looking for an opening.

Now it so chanced that Little John had fared expedi-
tiously with his errand. He had met the merchant, from
whom he was wont to buy Lincoln green, coming along
the road; and had made known his wants in a few words.
The merchant readily undertook to deliver the suits by a
certain day in the following month. So Little John, glad to
get back to the cool shelter of the greenwood, hasted along
the road lately taken by Robin.

Presently he heard the sound of angry voices, one of
which he recognized as his captain's.

"Now, Heaven forfend," quoth he, "that Robin Hood
has fallen into the clutches of a King's man! I must take
a peep at this fray."

So he cautiously made his way from tree to tree, as
Robin had done, till he came to the little open space
where Robin and Arthur were circling about each other
with angry looks, like two dogs at bay.

"Ha! this looks interesting!" muttered Little John to
himself, for he loved a good quarter-staff bout above anything else in the world, and was the best man at it in all
the greenwood. And he crawled quietly underneath a
friendly bush—much as he had done when Robin undertook to teach Will Scarlet a lesson—and chuckled softly
to himself and slapped his thigh and prepared to watch the
fight at his ease.

Indeed it was both exciting and laughable. You would have chuckled one moment and caught your breath the next, to see those two stout fellows swinging their sticks— each half as long again as the men were, and thick as their arm—and edging along sidewise, neither wishing to strike the first blow.

At last Robin could no longer forbear, and his good right arm swung round like a flash. Ping! went the stick on the back of the other's head, raising such a welt that the blood came. But the tanner did not seem to mind it at all, for bing! went his own staff in return, giving Robin as good as he had sent. Then the battle was on, and furiously it waged. Fast fell the blows, but few save the first ones landed, being met in midair by a counter-blow till the thwacking sticks sounded like the steady roll of a kettle-drum and the oak-bark flew as fine as it had ever done in Arthur-a-Bland's tannery.

Round and round they fought, digging their heels into the ground to keep from slipping, so that you would have vowed there had been a yoke of oxen ploughing a potato-patch. Round and round, up and down, in and out, their arms working like threshing-machines, went the yeoman and the tanner, for a full hour, each becoming more astonished every minute that the other was such a good fellow. While Little John from underneath his bushy covert had much ado to keep from roaring aloud in pure joy.

Finally Robin saw his chance and brought a full arm blow straight down upon the other's head with a force that would have felled a bullock. But Arthur's trebled cow-skin cap here stood him in good stead: the blow glanced off without doing more than stunning him. Nathless, he reeled and had much ado to keep from falling; seeing which Robin stayed his hand—to his own sorrow, for the tanner recovered his wits in a marvelous quick space and sent back a side-long blow which fairly lifted Robin off his feet and sent him tumbling on to the grass.

"Hold your hand! hold your hand!" roared Robin with what little breath he had left. "Hold, I say, and I will give you the freedom of the greenwood."

"Why, God-a-mercy," said Arthur; "I may thank my staff for that—not you."

"Well, well, gossip! let it be as it may. But prithee tell me your name and trade. I like to know fellows who can hit a blow like that same last."

"I am a tanner," replied Arthur-a-Bland. "In Nottingham long have I wrought. And if you'll come to me I swear I'll tan your hides for naught."

"Odds bodikins!" quoth Robin ruefully, "Mine own hide is tanned enough for the present. Howsoever, there be others in this wood I would fain see you tackle. Harkee, if you will leave your tan-pots and come with me, as sure as my name is Robin Hood, you shan't want gold or fee."

"By the breath o' my body!" said Arthur, "that will I do!" and he gripped him gladly by the hand. "But I am minded that I clean forgot the errand that brought me to Sherwood. I was commissioned by some, under the Sheriff's roof, to capture you."

"So was a certain tinker, now in our service," said Robin smilingly.

"Verily 'tis a new way to recruit forces!" said the tanner, laughing loudly. "But tell me, good Robin Hood, where is Little John? I fain would see him, for he is a kinsman on my mother's side."

"Here am I, good Arthur-a-Bland!" said a voice; and Little John literally rolled out from under the bush to the sward. His eyes were full of tears from much laughter which had well-nigh left him powerless to get on his feet.

As soon as the astonished tanner saw who it was, he gave Little John a mighty hug around the neck, and lifted him up on his feet, and the two pounded each other on the back soundly, so glad were they to meet again.

"O, man, man!" said Little John as soon as he had got his breath. "Never saw I so fine a fight in all my born days. You did knock him over like as he were a ninepin!"

"And you do joy to see me thwacked about on the ribs?" asked Robin with some choler.

"Nay, not that, master!" said Little John. "But 'tis the second time I have had special tickets to a show from beneath the bushes, and I cannot forbear my delight. Howsoever, take no shame unto yourself, for this same Arthur-a-Bland is the best man at the quarter-staff in all Nottinghamshire. It commonly takes two or three men to hold him."

"Unless it be Eric o' Lincoln," said Arthur modestly; "and I well know how you paid him out at the Fair."

"Say no more!" said Robin, springing to his feet; "for well I know that I have done good business this day, and a few bruises are easy payment for the stout cudgel I am getting into the band. Your hand again, good Arthur-a-

"By my troth, a gay bird!" (Page 73)

Bland! Come! let us after the deer of which I spoiled your stalking."

"Right gladly!" quoth Arthur. "Come, Cousin Little John! Away with vats and tanbark and vile-smelling cowhides! I'll follow you two in the sweet open air to the very ends of the earth!"

XVI

how Robin Hood Met Sir Richard of the Lea

Then answered him the gentle knight
With words both fair and free:
"God save thee, my good Robin,
And all thy company!"

Now you must know that some months passed by. The winter dragged its weary length through Sherwood Forest, and Robin Hood and his merry men found what cheer they could in the big crackling fires before their woodland cave. Friar Tuck had built him a little hermitage not far away, where he lived comfortably with his numerous dogs.

The winter, I say, reached an end at last, and the blessed spring came—and went. Another summer passed on apace, and still neither King nor Sheriff nor Bishop could catch the outlaws, who, meanwhile, thrived and prospered mightily in their outlawry. The band had been increased from time to time by picked men such as Arthur-a-Bland and David of Doncaster—he who was the jolliest cobbler for miles around—until it now numbered a full sevenscore of men; seven companies each with its stout lieutenant serving under bold Robin Hood. And

194

still they relieved the purses of the rich, and aided the poor, and feasted upon King's deer, until the lank Sheriff of Nottingham was well-nigh distracted.

Indeed, that official would probably have lost his office entirely, had it not been for the fact of the King's death. Henry passed away, as all kings will, in common with ordinary men, and Richard of the Lion Heart was proclaimed as his successor.

Then Robin and his men, after earnest debate, resolved to throw themselves upon the mercy of the new King, swear allegiance, and ask to be organized into Royal Foresters. So Will Scarlet and Will Stutely and Little John were sent to London with this message, which they were first to entrust privately to Maid Marian. But they soon returned with bad tidings. The new King had by now set forth upon a crusade to the Holy Land, and Prince John, his brother, was impossible to deal with— being crafty, cruel and treacherous. He was laying his hands upon all the property which could easily be seized; among other estates, that of the Earl of Huntingdon, Robin's old enemy and Marian's father, who had lately died.

Marian herself was in sore straits. Not only had her estates been taken away, and the maid been deprived of the former protection of the Queen, but the evil Prince John had persecuted her with his attentions. He thought that since the maid was defenseless he could carry her away to one of his castles and none could gainsay him.

No word of this peril reached Robin's ears, although his men brought him word of the seizure of the Huntingdon lands. Nathless, he was greatly alarmed for the safety of Maid Marian, and his heart cried out for her strongly. She had been continually in his thoughts ever since the memorable shooting at London town.

One morning in early autumn when the leaves were beginning to turn gold at the edges, the chestnut-pods to swell with promise of fatness, and the whole wide woodland was redolent with the ripe fragrance of fruit and flower, Robin was walking along the edge of a small open glade busy with his thoughts. The peace of the woods was upon him, despite his broodings of Marian, and he paid little heed to a group of does quietly feeding among the trees at the far edge of the glade.

But presently this sylvan picture was rudely disturbed for him. A stag, wild and furious, dashed suddenly forth from among the trees, scattering the does in swift alarm. The vicious beast eyed the green-and-gold tunic of Robin, and, lowering its head, charged at him impetuously. So sudden was its attack that Robin had no time to bend his bow. He sprang behind a tree while he seized his weapon.

A moment later the wild stag crashed blindly into the tree trunk with a shock which sent the beast reeling backwards, while the dislodged leaves from the shivering tree fell in a small shower over Robin's head.

"By my halidom, I am glad it was not me you struck, my gentle friend!" quoth Robin, fixing an arrow upon the string. "Sorry indeed would be any one's plight who should encounter you in this black humor."

Scarcely had he spoken when he saw the stag veer about and fix its glances rigidly on the bushes to the left side of the glade. These were parted by a delicate hand, and through the opening appeared the slight figure of a page. It was Maid Marian, come back again to the greenwood! She advanced, unconscious alike of Robin's horrified gaze and the evil fury of the stag.

She was directly in line with the animal, so Robin dared not launch an arrow. Her own bow was slung across her

shoulder, and her small sword would be useless against the beast's charge. But now as she caught sight of the stag she pursed her lips as though she would whistle to it.

"For the love of God, dear lady!" cried Robin; and then the words died in his throat.

With a savage snort of rage, the beast rushed at this new and inviting target—rushed so swiftly and from so short a distance that she could not defend herself. She sprang to one side as it charged down upon her, but a side blow from its antlers stretched her upon the ground. The stag stopped, turned, and lowered its head preparing to gore her to death.

Already its cruel horns were coming straight for her, while she, white of face and bewildered by the sudden attack, was struggling to rise and draw her sword. A moment more and the end would have come. But the sharp voice of Robin had already spoken.

"Down, Marian!" he cried, and the girl instinctively obeyed, just as the shaft from Robin's bow went whizzing close above her head and struck with terrific force full in the centre of the stag's forehead.

The beast stumbled in its charge and fell dead, across the body of the fainting maid.

Robin was quickly by her side, and dragged the beast from off the girl. Picking her up in his strong arms he bore her swiftly to the side of one of the many brooks which watered the vale.

He dashed cool water upon her face, roughly almost, in his agony of fear that she was already dead, and he could have shed tears of joy to see those poor, closed eyelids tremble. He redoubled his efforts; and presently she gave a little gasp.

"Where am I? What is 't?"

"You are in Sherwood, dear maid, tho', i' faith, we gave you a rude reception!"

She opened her eyes and sat up. "Methinks you have rescued me from sudden danger, sir," she said.

Then she recognized Robin for the first time, and a radiant smile came over her face, together with the rare blush of returned vitality, and her head sank upon his shoulder with a little tremble and sigh of relief.

"Oh, Robin, it is you!" she murmured.

"Aye, 'tis I. Thank heaven, I was at hand to do you service!" Robin's tones were deep and full of feeling. "I swear, dear Marian, that I will not let you from my care henceforth."

Not another word was spoken for some moments, while her head still rested confidently upon his breast. Then recollecting, he suddenly cried:

"Gramercy, I make but a poor nurse! I have not even asked if any of your bones are broken."

"No, not any," she answered springing lightly to her feet to show him. "That foolish dizziness o'ercame me for the nonce, but we can now proceed on our way."

"Nay, I meant not that," he protested; "why should we haste? First tell me of the news in London town, and of yourself."

So she told him how that the Prince had seized upon her father's lands, and had promised to restore them to her if she would listen to his suit; and how that she knew he meant her no good, for he was even then suing for a Princess's hand.

"That is all, Robin," she ended simply; "and that is why I donned again my page's costume and came to you in the greenwood."

Robin's brow had grown fiercely black at the recital of

her wrongs; and he had laid stern hand upon the hilt of his sword.

"By this sword which Queen Eleanor gave me!" he said impetuously; "and which was devoted to the service of all womankind, I take oath that Prince John and all his armies shall not harm you!"

So that is how Maid Marian came to take up her abode in the greenwood, where the whole band of yeomen welcomed her gladly and swore fealty; and where the sweet lady of Allan-a-Dale made her fully at home.

But this was a day of deeds in Sherwood Forest, and we 'gan to tell you of another happening which led to later events.

While Robin and Marian were having their encounter with the stag, Little John, Much the miller's son, and Will Scarlet had sallied forth to watch the highroad leading to Barnesdale, if perchance they might find some haughty knight or fat priest whose wallet needed lightening.

They had scarcely watched the great road known as Watling Street—which runs from Dover in Kent to Chester town—for many minutes, when they espied a knight riding by in a very forlorn and careless manner.

> All dreary was his semblance,
>   And little was his pride;
> His one foot in the stirrup stood,
>   His other waved beside.
>
> His visor hung down o'er his eyes,
>   He rode in single array,
> A sorrier man than he was one
>   Rode never in summer's day.

Little John came up to the knight and bade him stay; for who can judge of a man's wealth by his looks? The outlaw bent his knee in all courtesy, and prayed him to accept the hospitality of the forest.

"My master expects you to dine with him, to-day," quoth he, "and indeed has been fasting while awaiting your coming, these three hours."

"Who is your master?" asked the knight.

"None other than Robin Hood," replied Little John, laying his hand upon the knight's bridle.

Seeing the other two outlaws approaching, the knight shrugged his shoulders, and replied indifferently.

" 'Tis clear that your invitation is too urgent to admit of refusal," quoth he, "and I do go with you right willingly, my friends. My purpose was to have dined to-day at Blyth or Doncaster; but nothing matters greatly."

So in the same lackadaisical fashion which had marked all his actions that day, the knight suffered his horse to be led to the rendezvous of the band in the greenwood.

Marian had not yet had time to change her page's attire, when the three escorts of the knight hove in sight. She recognized their captive as Sir Richard of the Lea, whom she had often seen at court; and fearing lest he might recognize her, she would have fled. But Robin asked her, with a twinkle, if she would not like to play page that day, and she in roguish mood consented to do so.

"Welcome, Sir Knight," said Robin, courteously. "You are come in good time, for we were just preparing to sit down to meat."

"God save and thank you, good Master Robin," returned the knight; "and all your company. It likes me well to break the fast with you."

So while his horse was cared for, the knight laid aside his own heavy gear, and laved his face and hands, and sat down with Robin and all his men to a most plentiful repast

of venison, swans, pheasants, various small birds, cakes
and ale. And Marian stood behind Robin and filled his
cup and that of the guest.

After eating right heartily of the good cheer, the knight
brightened up greatly and vowed that he had not enjoyed
so good a dinner for nigh three weeks. He also said that
if ever Robin and his fellows should come to his domains,
he would strive to set them down to as good a dinner on
his own behalf.

But this was not exactly the sort of payment which
Robin had expected to receive. He thanked the knight,
therefore, in set phrase, but reminded him that a yeoman
like himself might hardly offer such a dinner to a knight
as a gift of charity.

"I have no money, Master Robin," answered the knight
frankly. "I have so little of the world's goods, in sooth,
that I should be ashamed to offer you the whole of it."

"Money, however little, always jingles merrily in our
pockets," said Robin, smiling. "Pray you tell me what you
deem a little sum."

"I have of my own ten silver pennies," said the knight.
"Here they are and I wish they were ten times as many."

He handed Little John his pouch, and Robin nodded
carelessly.

"What say you to the total, Little John?" he asked as
though in jest.

" 'Tis true enough, as the worthy knight hath said," responded the big fellow, gravely emptying the contents on
his cloak.

Robin signed to Marian, who filled a bumper of wine
for himself and his guest.

"Pledge me, Sir Knight!" cried the merry outlaw; "and

pledge me heartily, for these sorry times. I see that your armor is bent and that your clothes are torn. Yet methinks I saw you at court, once upon a day, and in more prosperous guise. Tell me now, were you a yeoman and made a knight by force? Or, have you been a bad steward to yourself, and wasted your property in lawsuits and the like? Be not bashful with us. We shall not betray your secrets."

"I am a Saxon knight in my own right; and I have always lived a sober and quiet life," the sorrowful guest replied. " 'Tis true you have seen me at court, mayhap, for I was an excited witness at your shooting before King Harry—God rest his bones! My name is Sir Richard of the Lea and I dwell in a castle, not a league from one of the gates of Nottingham, which has belonged to my father, and his father, and his father's father before him. Within two or three years ago my neighbors might have told you that a matter of four hundred pounds one way or the other was as naught to me. But now I have only these ten pennies of silver, and my wife and son."

"In what manner have you lost your riches?" asked Robin.

"Through folly and kindness," said the knight, sighing. "I went with King Richard upon a crusade, from which I am but lately returned, in time to find my son—a goodly youth—grown up. He was but twenty, yet he had achieved a squire's training and could play prettily in jousts and tournaments and other knightly games. But about this time he had the ill luck to push his sports too far, and did accidentally kill a knight in the open lists. To save the boy, I had to sell my lands and mortgage my ancestral castle; and this not being enough, in the end I have had to borrow money, at a ruinous interest, from my lord of Hereford."

"A most worthy Bishop," said Robin ironically. "What is the sum of your debt?"

"Four hundred pounds," said Sir Richard, "and the Bishop swears he will foreclose the mortgage if they are not paid promptly."

"Have you any friends who would become surety for you?"

"Not one. If good King Richard were here, the tale might be otherwise."

"Fill your goblet again, Sir Knight," said Robin; and he

turned to whisper a word in Marian's ear. She nodded
and drew Little John and Will Scarlet aside and talked
earnestly with them, in a low tone.

"Here is health and prosperity to you, gallant Robin,"
said Sir Richard, tilting his goblet. "I hope I may pay
your cheer more worthily, the next time I ride by."

Will Scarlet and Little John had meanwhile fallen in
with Marian's idea, for they consulted the other outlaws,
who nodded their heads. Thereupon Little John and
Will Scarlet went into the cave near by and presently returned bearing a bag of gold. This they counted out before the astonished knight; and there were four times one
hundred gold pieces in it.

"Take this loan from us, Sir Knight, and pay your debt

to the Bishop," then said Robin. "Nay, no thanks; you are but exchanging creditors. Mayhap we shall not be so hard upon you as the Christian Bishop; yet, again we may be harder. Who can tell?"

There were actual tears in Sir Richard's eyes, as he essayed to thank the foresters. But at this juncture, Much, the miller's son came from the cave dragging a bale of cloth.

"The knight should have a suit worthy of his rank, master—think you not so?"

"Measure him twenty good ells of it," ordered Robin.

"Give him a good horse, also," whispered Marian. "'Tis a gift which will come back fourfold, for this is a worthy man. I know him well."

So the horse was given, also, and Robin bade Arthur-a-Bland ride with the knight as far as his castle, as esquire.

The knight was sorrowful no longer; yet he could scarcely voice his thanks through his broken utterance. And having spent the night in rest, after listening to Allan-a-Dale's singing, he mounted his new steed the following morning an altogether different man.

"God save you, comrades, and keep you all!" said he, with deep feeling in his tones; "and give me a grateful heart!"

"We shall wait for you twelve months from to-day, here in this place," said Robin, shaking him by the hand; "and then you will repay us the loan, if you have been prospered."

"I shall return it to you within the year, upon my honor as Sir Richard of the Lea. And for all time, pray count on me as a steadfast friend."

So saying, the knight and his esquire rode down the forest glade till they were lost to view.

XVII

how The Bishop Was Dined

"O what is the matter?" then said the
    Bishop,
    "Or for whom do you make this
    a-do?
Or why do you kill the King's veni-
    son,
    When your company is so few?"

"We are shepherds," quoth bold Robin
    Hood,
    "And we keep sheep all the year,
And we are disposed to be merrie this
    day,
    And to kill the King's fat deer."

Not many days after Sir Richard of
the Lea came to Sherwood Forest, word reached Robin
Hood's ears that my lord Bishop of Hereford would be
riding that way betimes on that morning. 'Twas Arthur-
a-Bland, the knight's quondam esquire, who brought the
tidings, and Robin's face brightened as he heard it.

"Now, by our Lady!" quoth he, "I have long desired
to entertain my lord in the greenwood, and this is too
fair a chance to let slip. Come, my men, kill me a veni-

son; kill me a good fat deer. The Bishop of Hereford is to dine with me to-day, and he shall pay well for his cheer."

"Shall we dress it here, as usual?" asked Much, the miller's son.

"Nay, we will play a droll game on the churchman. We will dress it by the highway side, and watch for the Bishop narrowly, lest he should ride some other way."

So Robin gave his orders, and the main body of his men dispersed to different parts of the forest, under Will Stutely and Little John, to watch other roads; while Robin Hood himself took six of his men, including Will Scarlet, and Much, and posted himself in full view of the main road. This little company appeared funny enough, I assure you, for they had disguised themselves as shepherds. Robin had an old wool cap, with a tail to it, hanging over his ear, and a shock of hair stood straight up through a hole in the top. Besides there was so much dirt on his face that you would never have known him. An old tattered cloak over his hunter's garb completed his make-up. The others were no less ragged and unkempt, even the foppish Will Scarlet being so badly run down at the heel that the court ladies would hardly have had speech with him.

They quickly provided themselves with a deer and made great preparations to cook it over a small fire, when a little dust was seen blowing along the highway, and out of it came the portly Bishop cantering along on a white nag with ten men-at-arms at his heels. As soon as he saw the fancied shepherds he spurred up his horse, and came straight toward them.

"Who are ye, fellows, who make so free with the King's deer?" he asked sharply.

Louis Slobodkin

"We are shepherds," answered Robin Hood, pulling at his forelock awkwardly.

"Heaven have mercy! Ye seem a sorry lot of shepherds. But who gave you leave to cease eating mutton?"

" 'Tis one of our feast days, lording, and we were disposed to be merry this day, and make free with a deer, out here where they be so many."

"By my faith, the King shall hear of this. Who killed yon beast?"

"Give me first your name, excellence, so that I may speak where 'tis fitting," replied Robin stubbornly.

" 'Tis my lord Bishop of Hereford, fellow!" interposed one of the guards fiercely. "See that you keep a civil tongue in your head."

"If 'tis a churchman," retorted Will Scarlet, "he would do better to mind his own flocks rather than concern himself with ours."

"Ye are saucy fellows, in sooth," cried the Bishop, "and we will see if your heads will pay for your manners. Come! quit your stolen roast and march along with me, for you shall be brought before the Sheriff of Nottingham forthwith."

"Pardon, excellence!" said Robin, dropping on his knees. "Pardon, I pray you. It becomes not your lordship's coat to take so many lives away."

"Faith, I'll pardon you!" said the Bishop. "I'll pardon you, when I see you hanged! Seize upon them, my men!"

His bodyguard lost no time in striving to put this curt order into effect.

But Robin had already sprung away with his back against a tree. And from underneath his ragged cloak he drew his trusty horn and winded the piercing notes which were wont to summon the band.

The Bishop no sooner saw this action than he knew his man, and that there was a trap set; and being an arrant coward, he wheeled his horse sharply and would have made off down the road; but his own men, spurred on the charge, blocked his way. At almost the same instant the bushes round about seemed literally to become alive with outlaws. Little John's men came from one side and Will Stutely's from the other. In less time than it takes to tell it, the worthy Bishop was taken off his white nag and found himself a prisoner. At first he stormed and blustered; then almost in the same breath he began to crave mercy from the men he had so lately been ready to sentence.

> "O pardon, O pardon," said the Bishop,
> "O pardon I you pray.
> For if I had known it had been you,
> I'd have gone some other way."

"I owe you no pardon," retorted Robin, "but I will e'en treat you better than you would have treated me. Come, make haste, and go along with me. I have already planned that you shall dine with me this day."

So the unwilling prelate was dragged away, cheek by jowl, with the half-cooked venison upon the back of his own horse; and Robin and his band took charge of the whole company and led them through the forest glades till they came to an open space near Barnesdale.

Here they rested, and Robin gave the Bishop a seat full courteously. Much the miller's son fell to roasting the deer afresh, while another and fatter beast was set to frizzle on the other side of the fire. Presently the appetizing odor of the cooking reached the Bishop's nostrils, and he sniffed it eagerly. The morning's ride had made him hungry; and he was nothing loath when they bade him come to dinner. Robin gave him the best place beside himself, and the Bishop prepared to fall to.

"Nay, my lord, craving your pardon, but we are accustomed to have grace before meat," said Robin decorously. "And as our own chaplain is not with us to-day, will you be good enough to say it for us?"

The Bishop reddened, but pronounced grace in the Latin tongue hastily, and then settled himself to make the best of his lot. Red wines and ale were brought forth and poured out, each man having a horn tankard from which to drink.

Laughter bubbled among the diners, and the Bishop caught himself smiling at more than one jest. But who, in sooth, could resist a freshly broiled venison steak eaten out in the open air to the tune of jest and good fellowship? Stutely filled the Bishop's beaker with wine each time he emptied it, and the Bishop got mellower and mellower as the afternoon shades lengthened on toward sunset. Then the approaching dusk warned him of his position.

"I wish, mine host," quoth he gravely to Robin, who had soberly drunk but one cup of ale, "that you would now call a reckoning. 'Tis late, and I fear the cost of this entertainment may be more than my poor purse can stand."

For he bethought himself of his friend the Sheriff's former experience.

"Verily, your lordship," said Robin, scratching his head, "I have enjoyed your company so much, that I scarce know how to charge for it."

"Lend me your purse, my lord," said Little John, interposing, "and I'll give you the reckoning by and by."

The Bishop shuddered. He had collected Sir Richard's debt only that morning, and was even then carrying it home.

"I have but a few silver pennies of my own," he whined; "and as for the gold in my saddle-bags, 'tis for the church. Ye surely would not levy upon the church, my good friends."

But Little John was already gone to the saddle-bags, and returning he laid the Bishop's cloak upon the ground, and poured out of the portmanteau a matter of four hundred glittering gold pieces. 'Twas the identical money which Robin had lent Sir Richard a short while before!

"Ah!" said Robin, as though an idea had but just then come to him. "The church is always willing to aid in charity. And seeing this goodly sum reminds me that I have a friend who is indebted to a churchman for this exact amount. Now we shall charge you nothing on our own account; but suffer us to make use of this in aiding my good friend."

"Nay, nay," began the Bishop with a wry face, "this is requiting me ill indeed. Was this not the King's meat, after all, that we feasted upon? Furthermore, I am a poor man."

"Poor, forsooth!" answered Robin in scorn. "You are the Bishop of Hereford, and does not the whole countryside speak of your oppression? Who does not know of your cruelty to the poor and ignorant—you who should use your great office to aid them, instead of oppress? Have you not been guilty of far greater robbery than this, even though less open? Of myself, and how you have pursued me, I say nothing; nor of your unjust enmity against my father. But on account of those you have despoiled and oppressed, I take this money, and will use it far more worthily than you would. God be my witness in this! There is an end of the matter, unless you will lead us in a song or dance to show that your body has a better spirit than your mind. Come, strike up the harp, Allan!"

"Neither the one nor the other will I do," snarled the Bishop.

"Faith, then we must help you," said Little John; and he and Arthur-a-Bland seized the fat, struggling churchman and commenced to hop up and down. The Bishop being shorter must perforce accompany them in their gyrations; while the whole company sat and rolled about over the ground, and roared to see my lord of Hereford's queer capers. At last he sank in a heap, fuddled with wine and quite exhausted.

Little John picked him up as though he were a log of wood and carrying him to his horse, set him astride facing the animal's tail; and thus fastened him, leading the animal toward the highroad and, starting the Bishop, more dead than alive, toward Nottingham.

The churchman, howbeit, was so glad to escape the clutches of these merry men of the forest, that he cared little how he fared forth. 'Twas a picture which made strange contrast to the bold prelate who rode up in the morning.

XVIII

how The Bishop Went Outlaw Hunting

The Bishop he came to the old wom-
    an's house,
And called with furious mood,
"Come let me soon see, and bring unto
    me
That traitor, Robin Hood."

THE easy success with which they
had got the better of the good Bishop led Robin to grow a
little careless. He thought that his guest was too great a
coward to venture back into the greenwood for many
a long day; and so after lying quiet for one day, the outlaw ventured boldly upon the highway, the morning of
the second. But he had gone only half a mile when, turning a sharp bend in the road, he plunged full upon the
prelate himself.

My lord of Hereford had been so deeply smitten in his
pride, that he had lost no time in summoning a consider-
able body of the Sheriff's men, offering to double the reward if Robin Hood could be come upon. This company
was now at his heels, and after the first shock of mutual
surprise, the Bishop gave an exultant shout and spurred
upon the outlaw.

216

It was too late for Robin to retreat by the way he had come, but quick as a flash he sprang to one side of the road, dodged under some bushes, and disappeared so suddenly that his pursuers thought he had truly been swallowed up by magic.

"After him!" yelled the Bishop; "some of you beat up the woods around him, while the rest of us will keep on the main road and head him off on the other side!"

For, truth to tell, the Bishop did not care to trust his bones away from the highroad.

About a mile away, on the other side of this neck of woods, wherein Robin had been trapped, was a little tumbledown cottage. 'Twas where the widow lived, whose three sons had been rescued. Robin remembered the cottage and saw his one chance to escape.

Doubling in and out among the underbush and heather with the agility of a hare, he soon came out of the wood in the rear of the cottage, and thrust his head through a tiny window.

The widow, who had been at her spinning-wheel, rose up with a cry of alarm.

"Quiet, good mother! 'Tis I, Robin Hood. Where are your three sons?"

"They should be with you, Robin. Well do you know that. Do they not owe their lives to you?"

"If that be so, I come to seek payment of the debt," said Robin in a breath. "The Bishop is on my heels with many of his men."

"I'll cheat the Bishop and all!" cried the woman quickly. "Here, Robin, change your raiment with me, and we will see if my lord knows an old woman when he sees her."

"Good!" said Robin. "Pass your gray cloak out the window, and also your spindle and twine; and I will give you my green mantle and everything else down to my bow and arrows."

While they had been talking, Robin had been nimbly changing clothes with the old woman, through the window, and in a jiffy he stood forth complete, even to the spindle and twine.

Presently up dashed the Bishop and his men, and, at sight of the cottage and the old woman, gave pause.

"Now by all the saints"—began the Bishop—"we shall see if the rascally outlaw escapes our clutches this time."

The crone was hobbling along with difficulty, leaning heavily upon a gnarled stick and bearing the spindle on her other arm. She would have gone by the Bishop's company, while muttering to herself, but the Bishop ordered one of his men to question her. The soldier laid his hand upon her shoulder.

"Mind your business!" croaked the woman, "or I'll curse ye!"

"Come, come, my good woman," said the soldier, who really was afraid of her curses. "I'll not molest you. But my lord Bishop of Hereford wants to know if you have seen aught of the outlaw, Robin Hood?"

"And why shouldn't I see him?" she whined. "Where's the King or law to prevent good Robin from coming to see me and bring me food and raiment? That's more than my lord Bishop will do, I warrant ye!"

"Peace, woman!" said the Bishop harshly. "We want none of your opinions. But we'll take you to Barnesdale and burn you for a witch if you do not instantly tell us when you last saw Robin Hood."

"Mercy, good my lord!" chattered the crone, falling on her knees. "Robin is there in my cottage now, but you'll never take him alive."

Louis Slobodkin

"We'll see about that," cried the Bishop triumphantly. "Enter the cottage, my men. Fire it, if need be. But I'll give a purse of gold pieces, above the reward, to the man who captures the outlaw alive."

The old woman, being released, went on her way slowly. But it might have been noticed that the farther she got away from the company and the nearer to the edge of the woods, the swifter and straighter grew her pace. Once inside the shelter of the forest she broke into a run of surprising swiftness.

"Gadzooks!" exclaimed Little John who presently spied her. "Who comes here? Never saw I witch or woman run so fast. Methinks I'll send an arrow close over her head to see which it is."

"O hold your hand! hold your hand!" panted the supposed woman. " 'Tis I, Robin Hood. Summon the yeomen and return with me speedily. We have still another score to settle with my lord of Hereford."

When Little John could catch his breath from laughing, he winded his horn.

"Now, mistress Robin," quoth he, grinning. "Lead on! We'll be close to your heels."

Meanwhile, back at the widow's cottage the Bishop was growing more furious every moment. For all his bold words, he dared not fire the house, and the sturdy door had thus far resisted all his men's efforts.

"Break it down! Break it down!" he shouted, "and let me soon see who will fetch out that traitor, Robin Hood!"

At last the door crashed in and the men stood guard at the threshold. But not one dared enter for fear a sharp arrow should meet him halfway.

"Here he is!" cried one keen-eyed fellow, peering in. "I

see him in the corner by the cupboard. Shall we slay him with our pikes?"

"Nay," said the Bishop, "take him alive if you can. We'll make the biggest public hanging of this that the shire ever beheld."

But the joy of the Bishop over his capture was short lived. Down the road came striding the shabby figure of the old woman who had helped him set the trap; and very wrathy was she when she saw that the cottage door had been battered in sunder.

"Stand by, you lazy rascals!" she called to the soldiers. "May all the devils catch ye for hurting an old woman's hut. Stand by, I say!"

"Hold your tongue!" ordered the Bishop. "These are my men and carrying out my orders."

"God-a-mercy!" swore the beldame harshly. "Things have come to a pretty pass when our homes may be treated like common gaols. Couldn't all your men catch one poor forester without this ado? Come! clear out, you and your robbers, on the instant, or I'll curse every mother's son of ye, eating and drinking and sleeping!"

"Seize on the hag!" shouted the Bishop, as soon as he could get in a word. "We'll see about a witch's cursing. Back to town she shall go, alongside of Robin Hood."

"Not so fast, your worship!" she retorted, clapping her hands.

And at the signal a goodly array of greenwood men sprang forth from all sides of the cottage, with bows drawn back threateningly. The Bishop saw that his men were trapped again, for they dared not stir. Nathless, he determined to make a fight for it.

"If one of you but budge an inch toward me, you ras-

cals," he cried, "it shall sound the death of your master,
Robin Hood! My men have him here under their pikes,
and I shall command them to kill him without mercy."

"Faith, I should like to see the Robin you have caught,"
said a clear voice from under the widow's cape; and the
outlaw chief stood forth with bared head smilingly. "Here
am I, my lord, in no wise imperilled by your men's fierce
pikes. So let us see whom you have been guarding so
well."

The old woman who, in the garb of Robin Hood, had
been lying quiet in the cottage through all the uproar,

jumped up nimbly at this. In the bald absurdity of her
disguise she came to the doorway and bowed to the
Bishop.

"Give you good-den, my lord Bishop," she piped in a
shrill voice; "and what does your Grace at my humble
door? Do you come to bless me and give me alms?"

"Aye, that does he," answered Robin. "We shall see
if his saddle-bags contain enough to pay you for that
battered door."

"Now by all the saints——" began the Bishop.

"Take care; they are all watching you," interrupted

Robin; "so name them not upon your unchurchly lips.
But I will trouble you to hand over that purse of gold you
had saved to pay for my head."

"I'll see you hanged first!" raged the Bishop, stating no
more than what would have been so, if he could have had
the ordering of things. "Have at them, my men, and hew
them down in their tracks!"

"Hold!" retorted Robin. "See how we have you at our
mercy." And aiming a sudden shaft he shot so close to the
Bishop's head that it carried away both his hat and the
skull-cap which he always wore, leaving him quite bald.

The prelate turned as white as his shiny head and
clutched wildly at his ears. He thought himself dead
almost.

"Help! Murder!" he gasped. "Do not shoot again!
What do ye want with me?"

"That will we decide in solemn council in the forest
hard by," said Robin grimly. "Come, my merry men!"

The outlaws, nothing loath and seeing sport ahead,
closed in around the unwilling Bishop and his men. The
latter were quickly disarmed; and the whole party proceeded to an open glade in the wood. Here Robin seated
himself upon the gnarled root of an oak tree, and bade the
Bishop stand before him.

"My lord Bishop," he said. "Meseems that one visit
from you does not satisfy. You repay your calls all too
promptly. Now what little gift have you for us before
you go on your way?"

While the Bishop pondered over his next words, as well
he might, Will Stutely came forward grinning broadly.

"Master," he said, "here's a merry game. We laid hold
of an old Jew's money-bags this very day, who swears by

all the patriarchs that his bags are empty. The Bishop, he says, levied unjust tribute upon him."

"Bring him forward," said Robin; and up came the Jew, a bent old man, cringing and whining.

"Mercy, good sirs!" he quavered. " 'Tis as this good yeoman has told you. My purse was seized by the Bishop's men."

"What would you give to have it restored to you?" asked Robin.

"The half of it willingly," said the Jew.

"How much was in your bag?"

"A full hundred pounds of gold."

"Then my lord Bishop," said Robin, "you can pay back to the Jew his hundred pounds and to us another hundred pounds for all the trouble you have caused this day."

" 'Tis more than I have by me," mumbled the Bishop.

"Ah," said Robin, "the church is always willing to aid in charity. Give this Jew a written order for the sum required, or your debt to us will be doubled."

And, to make a long story short, that is just what the worthy Bishop did.

XIX

how The Sheriff
Held Another
Shooting Match

"To tell the truth, I'm well informed
Yon match it is a wile;
The Sheriff, I wis, devises this
Us archers to beguile."

Now the Sheriff was so greatly
troubled in heart over the growing power of Robin Hood,
that he did a very foolish thing. He went to London town
to lay his troubles before the King and get another force of
troops to cope with the outlaws. King Richard was not
yet returned from the Holy Land, but Prince John heard
him with scorn.

"Pooh!" said he, shrugging his shoulders. "What have
I to do with all this? Art thou not sheriff for me? The law
is in force to take thy course of them that injure thee. Go,
get thee gone, and by thyself devise some tricking game to
trap these rebels; and never let me see thy face at court
again until thou hast a better tale to tell."

So away went the Sheriff in sorrier pass than ever, and
cudgeled his brain, on the way home, for some plan of
action.

His daughter met him on his return and saw at once that
226

he had been on a poor mission. She was minded to up-braid him when she learned what he had told the Prince. But the words of the latter started her to thinking afresh.

"I have it!" she exclaimed at length. "Why should we not hold another shooting-match? 'Tis Fair year, as you know, and another tourney will be expected. Now we will proclaim a general amnesty, as did King Harry himself, and say that the field is open and unmolested to all comers. Belike Robin Hood's men will be tempted to twang the bow, and then——"

"And then," said the Sheriff jumping up with alacrity, "we will see on which side of the gate they stop over-night!"

So the Sheriff lost no time in proclaiming a tourney, to be held that same fall at the Fair. It was open to all comers, said the proclamation, and none should be mo-lested in their going and coming. Furthermore, an arrow with a golden head and shaft of silver-white should be given to the winner, who would be heralded abroad as the finest archer in all the North Countree. Also, many rich prizes were to be given to other clever archers.

These tidings came in due course to Robin Hood, under the greenwood tree, and fired his impetuous spirit.

"Come, prepare ye, my merry men all," quoth he, "and we'll go to the Fair and take some part in this sport."

With that stepped forth the merry cobbler, David of Doncaster. "Master," quoth he, "be ruled by me and stir not from the greenwood. To tell the truth, I'm well in-formed yon match is naught but a trap. I wis the Sheriff has devised it to beguile us archers into some treachery."

"That word savors of the coward," replied Robin, "and pleases me not. Let come what will, I'll try my skill at that same archery."

LOUIS Slobodkin

Then up spoke Little John and said: "Come, listen to me how it shall be that we will not be discovered.

"Our mantles all of Lincoln-green
Behind us we will leave;
We'll dress us all so several,
They shall not us perceive.

"One shall wear white, another red,
One yellow, another blue;
Thus in disguise to the exercise
We'll go, whate'er ensue."

This advice met with general favor from the adventurous fellows, and they lost no time in putting it into practice. Maid Marian and Mistress Dale, assisted by Friar Tuck, prepared some vari-colored costumes, and 'gainst the Fair day had fitted out the sevenscore men till you would never have taken them for other than villagers decked for the holiday.

And forth went they from the greenwood, with hearts all firm and stout, resolved to meet the Sheriff's men and have a merry bout. Along the highway they fell in with many other bold fellows from the countryside, going with their ruddy-cheeked lasses toward the wide-open gates of Nottingham.

So in through the gates trooped the whole gay company, Robin's men behaving as awkwardly and laughing and

talking as noisily as the rest; while the Sheriff's scowling
men-at-arms stood round about and sought to find one
who looked like a forester, but without avail.

The herald now set forth the terms of the contest, as on
former occasions, and the shooting presently began.
Robin had chosen five of his men to shoot with him, and
the rest were to mingle with the crowd and also watch the
gates. These five were Little John, Will Scarlet, Will
Stutely, Much, and Allan-a-Dale.

The other competitors made a brave showing on the
first round, especially Gilbert of the White Hand, who was
present and never shot better. The contest later narrowed
down between Gilbert and Robin. But at the first lead,
when the butts were struck so truly by various well-known
archers, the Sheriff was in doubt whether to feel glad or
sorry. He was glad to see such skill, but sorry that the outlaws were not in it.

> Some said, "If Robin Hood were here,
>   And all his men to boot,
> Sure none of them could pass these men,
>   So bravely do they shoot."
>
> "Aye," quoth the Sheriff, and scratched his head,
>   "I thought he would be here;
> I thought he would, but tho' he's bold,
>   He durst not now appear."

This word was privately brought to Robin by David of
Doncaster, and the saying vexed him sorely. But he bit
his lip in silence.

"Ere long," he thought to himself, "we shall see whether
Robin Hood be here or not!"

Meantime the shooting had been going forward, and
Robin's men had done so well that the air was filled with
shouts.

One cried, "Blue jacket!" another cried, "Brown!"
And a third cried, "Brave Yellow!"
But the fourth man said, "Yon man in red
In his place has no fellow."

For that was Robin Hood himself,
For he was clothed in red;
At every shot the prize he got,
For he was both sure and dead.

Thus went the second round of the shooting, and thus the third and last, till even Gilbert of the White Hand was fairly beaten. During all this shooting, Robin exchanged no word with his men, each treating the other as a perfect stranger. Nathless, such great shooting could not pass without revealing the archers.

The Sheriff thought he discovered, in the winner of the golden arrow, the person of Robin Hood without peradventure. So he sent word privately for his men-at-arms to close round the group. But Robin's men also got wind of the plan.

To keep up appearances, the Sheriff summoned the crowd to form in a circle; and after as much delay as possible the arrow was presented. The delay gave time enough for the soldiers to close in. As Robin received his prize, bowed awkwardly and turned away, the Sheriff, letting his zeal get the better of his discretion, grasped him about the neck and called upon his men to arrest the traitor. But the moment the Sheriff touched Robin, he received such a buffet on the side of his head that he let go instantly and fell back several paces. Turning to see who had struck him, he recognized Little John.

"Ah, rascal Greenleaf, I have you now!" he exclaimed springing at him. Just then, however, he met a new check.

"This is from another of your devoted servants!" said a

voice which he knew to be that of Much the miller's son; and "Thwack!" went his open palm upon the Sheriff's cheek, sending that worthy rolling over and over upon the ground.

By this time the conflict had become general, but the Sheriff's men suffered the disadvantage of being hampered by the crowd of innocent onlookers, whom they could not tell from the outlaws and so dared not attack; while the other outlaws in the rear fell upon them and put them in confusion.

For a moment a fierce rain of blows ensued; then the clear bugle-note from Robin ordered a retreat. The two warders at the nearest gate tried to close it, but were shot dead in their tracks. David of Doncaster threw a third soldier into the moat; and out through the gate went the foresters in good order, keeping a respectful distance between themselves and the advancing soldiery, by means of their well-directed shafts.

But the fight was not to go easily this day, for the soldiery, smarting from their recent discomfiture at the widow's cottage, and knowing that the eyes of the whole shire were upon them, fought well, and pressed closely after the retreating outlaws. More than one ugly wound was given and received. No less than five of the Sheriff's men were killed outright, and a dozen others injured; while four of Robin's men were bleeding from severe flesh cuts.

Then Little John, who had fought by the side of his chief, suddenly fell forward with a slight moan. An arrow had pierced his knee. Robin seized the big fellow with almost superhuman strength.

> Up he took him on his back,
>   And bare him well a mile;
> Many a time he laid him down,
>   And shot another while.

Meanwhile Little John grew weaker and closed his eyes; at last he sank to the ground, and feebly motioned Robin to let him lie.

"Master Robin," said he, "have I not served you well, ever since we met upon the bridge?"

"Truer servant never man had," answered Robin.

"Then if ever you loved me, and for the sake of that service, draw your bright brown sword and strike off my head; never let me fall alive into the hand of the Sheriff of Nottingham."

"Not for all the gold in England would I do either of the things you suggest."

"God forbid!" cried Arthur-a-Bland, hurrying to the rescue. And, packing his wounded kinsman upon his own broad shoulders, he soon brought him within the shelter of the forest.

Once there, the Sheriff's men dared not follow; and Robin caused litters of boughs to be made for Little John and the other four wounded men. Quickly were they carried through the wood until the hermitage of Friar Tuck was reached, where their wounds were dressed. Little John's hurt was pronounced to be the most serious of any, but he was assured that in two or three week's time he could get about again; whereat the active giant groaned mightily.

That evening consternation came upon the hearts of the band. A careful roll-call was taken to see if all the yeomen had escaped, when it was found that Will Stutely was missing, and Maid Marian also was nowhere to be found. Robin was seized with dread. He knew that Marian had gone to the Fair, but felt that she would hardly come to grief. Her absence, however, portended some danger, and he feared that it was connected with Will Stutely.

The Sheriff would hang him speedily and without mercy, if he were captured.

The rest of the band shared their leader's uneasiness, though they said no word. They knew that if Will were captured, the battle must be fought over again the next day, and Will must be saved at any cost. But no man flinched from the prospect.

That evening, while the Sheriff and his wife and daughter sat at meat in the Mansion House, the Sheriff boasted of how he would make an example of the captured outlaw; for Stutely had indeed fallen into his hands.

"He shall be strung high," he said, in a loud voice; "and none shall dare lift a finger. I now have Robin Hood's men on the run, and we shall soon see who is master in this shire. I am only sorry that we let them have the golden arrow."

As he spoke a missive sped through a window and fell clattering upon his plate, causing him to spring back in alarm.

It was the golden arrow, and on its feathered shaft was sewed a little note which read:

"This is from one who will take no gifts from liars; and who henceforth will show no mercy. Look well to yourself. R.H."

XX

how Will Stutely Was Rescued

Forth of the greenwood are they gone,
Yea, all courageously,
Resolving to bring Stutely home,
Or every man to die.

THE next day dawned bright and sunny. The whole face of nature seemed gay as in despite of the tragedy which was soon to take place in the walls of Nottingham town. The gates were not opened upon this day, for the Sheriff was determined to carry through the hanging of Will Stutely undisturbed. No man, therefore, was to be allowed entrance from without, all that morning and until after the fatal hour of noon, when Will's soul was to be launched into eternity.

Early in the day Robin had drawn his men to a point, as near as he dared, in the woods where he could watch the road leading to the East gate. He himself was clad in a bright scarlet dress, while his men, a goodly array, wore their suits of sober Lincoln green. They were armed with broadswords, and each man carried his bow and a full quiver of new arrows, straightened and sharpened cunningly by Middle, the tinker. Over their greenwood dress, each man had thrown a rough mantle, making him look not unlike a friar.

236

"I hold it good, comrades," then said Robin Hood, "to tarry here in hiding for a season while we send someone forth to obtain tidings. For, in sooth, 'twill work no good to march upon the gates if they be closed."

"Look, master," quoth one of the widow's sons, "There comes a palmer along the road from the town. Belike he can tell us how the land lies, and if Stutely be really in jeopardy. Shall I go out and engage him in speech?"

"Go," answered Robin.

So Stout Will went out from the band while the others hid themselves and waited. When he had come close to the palmer, who seemed a slight, youngish man, he doffed his hat full courteously and said:

"I crave your pardon, holy man, but can you tell me tidings of Nottingham town? Do they intend to put an outlaw to death this day?"

"Yea," answered the palmer sadly. " 'Tis true enough, sorry be the day. I have passed the very spot where the gallows-tree is going up. 'Tis out upon the roadway near the Sheriff's castle. One, Will Stutely, is to be hung thereon at noon, and I could not bear the sight, so came away."

The palmer spoke in a muffled voice; and as his hood was pulled well over his head, Stout Will could not discern what manner of man he was. Over his shoulder he carried a long staff, with the fashion of a little cross at one end; and he had sandaled feet like any monk. Stout Will noticed idly that the feet were very small and white, but gave no second thought to the matter.

"Who will shrive the poor wretch, if you have come away from him?" he asked, reproachfully.

The question seemed to put a new idea into the palmer's

head. He turned so quickly that he almost dropped his hood.

"Do you think that I should undertake this holy office?"

"By Saint Peter and the Blessed Virgin, I do indeed! Else, who will do it? The Bishop and all his whining clerks may be there, but not one would say a prayer for his soul."

"But I am only a poor palmer," the other began hesitatingly.

"Nathless, your prayers are as good as any and better than some," replied Will.

"Right gladly would I go," then said the palmer; "but I fear me I cannot get into the city. You may know that the gates are fast locked, for this morning, for all who would come in, although they let any pass out who will."

"Come with me," said Stout Will, "and my master will see that you pass through the gates."

So the palmer pulled his cloak still closer about him and was brought before Robin Hood, to whom he told all he knew of the situation. He ended with:

"If I may make so bold, I would not try to enter the city from this gate, as 'tis closely guarded since yesterday. But on the far side, no attack is looked for."

"My thanks, gentle palmer," quoth Robin, "your suggestion is good, and we will deploy to the gate upon the far side."

So the men marched silently but quickly until they were near to the western gate. Then Arthur-a-Bland asked leave to go ahead as a scout, and quietly made his way to a point under the tower by the gate. The moat was dry on this side, as these were times of peace, and Arthur was further favored by a stout ivy vine which grew out from an upper window.

Swinging himself up boldly by means of this friendly vine, he crept through the window and in a moment more had sprung upon the warder from behind and gripped him hard about the throat. The warder had no chance to utter the slightest sound, and soon lay bound and gagged upon the floor, while Arthur-a-Bland slipped himself into his uniform and got hold of his keys.

'Twas the work of but a few moments more to open the gates, let down the bridge, and admit the rest of the band; and they got inside the town so quietly that none knew of their coming. Fortune also favored them in the fact that just at this moment the prison doors had been opened for the march of the condemned man, and every soldier and idle lout in the market-place had trooped thither to see him pass along.

Presently out came Will Stutely with firm step but dejected air. He looked eagerly to the right hand and to the left, but saw none of the band. And though more than one curious face betrayed friendship in it, he knew there could be no aid from such source.

Will's hands were tied behind his back. He marched between rows of soldiery, and the Sheriff and the Bishop brought up the rear on horses, looking mightily puffed up and important over the whole proceeding. He would show these sturdy rebels—would the Sheriff—whose word was law! He knew that the gates were tightly fastened; and further he believed that the outlaws would hardly venture again within the walls, even if the gates were open. And as he looked around at fivescore archers and pike-men who lined the way to the gallows, he smiled with grim satisfaction.

Seeing that no help was nigh, the prisoner paused at

the foot of the scaffold and spoke in a firm tone to the Sheriff.

"My lord Sheriff," quoth he, "since I must needs die, grant me one boon; for my noble master ne'er yet had a man that was hanged on a tree:

> "Give me a sword all in my hand,
>   And let me be unbound,
> And with thee and thy men will I fight
>   Till I lie dead on the ground."

But the Sheriff would by no means listen to his request; but swore that he should be hanged a shameful death, and not die by the sword valiantly.

> "O no, no, no," the Sheriff said,
>   "Thou shalt on the gallows die,
> Aye, and so shall thy master too,
>   If ever it in me lie."

> "O dastard coward!" Stutely cried,
>   "Faint-hearted peasant slave!
> If ever my master do thee meet,
>   Thou shalt thy payment have.

> "My noble master thee doth scorn,
>   And all thy cowardly crew;
> Such silly imps unable are
>   Bold Robin to subdue."

This brave speech was not calculated to soothe the Sheriff. "To the gallows with him!" he roared, giving a sign to the hangman; and Stutely was pushed into the rude cart which was to bear him under the gallows until his neck was leashed. Then the cart would be drawn roughly away and the unhappy man would swing out over the tail of it into another world.

At this moment came a slight interruption. A boyish-looking palmer stepped forth, and said:

"Your Excellency, let me at least shrive this poor wretch's soul ere it be hurled into eternity."

"No!" shouted the Sheriff, "let him die a dog's death!"

"Then his damnation will rest upon you," said the monk firmly. "You, my lord Bishop, cannot stand by and see this wrong done."

The Bishop hesitated. Like the Sheriff, he wanted no delay; but the people were beginning to mutter among themselves and move about uneasily. He said a few words to the Sheriff, and the latter nodded to the monk ungraciously.

"Perform your duty, Sir Priest," quoth he, "and be quick about it!" Then, turning to his soldiers, "Watch this palmer narrowly," he commanded. "Belike he is in league with those rascally outlaws."

But the palmer paid no heed to his last words. He began to tell his beads quickly, and to speak in a low voice to the condemned man. But he did not touch his bonds.

Then came another stir in the crowd, and one came pushing through the press of people and soldiery to come near to the scaffold.

"I pray you, Will, before you die, take leave of all your friends!" cried out the well-known voice of Much, the miller's son.

At the word the palmer stepped back suddenly and looked to one side. The Sheriff also knew the speaker.

"Seize him!" he shouted. " 'Tis another of the crew. He is the villain cook who once did rob me of my silver plate. We'll make a double hanging of this!"

"Not so fast, good master Sheriff," retorted Much. "First catch your man and then hang him. But meanwhile I would like to borrow my friend of you awhile."

And with one stroke of his keen hunting-knife he cut the bonds which fastened the prisoner's arms, and Stutely leaped lightly from the cart.

"Treason!" screamed the Sheriff, getting black with rage. "Catch the varlets!"

So saying he spurred his horse fiercely forward, and rising in his stirrups brought down his sword with might and main at Much's head. But his former cook dodged nimbly underneath the horse and came up on the other side, while the weapon whistled harmlessly in the air.

"Nay, Sir Sheriff!" he cried, "I must e'en borrow your sword for the friend I have borrowed."

Thereupon he snatched the weapon deftly from the Sheriff's hand.

"Here, Stutely!" said he, "the Sheriff has lent you his own sword. Back to back with me, man, and we'll teach these knaves a trick or two!"

Meanwhile the soldiers had recovered from their momentary surprise and had flung themselves into the fray. A clear bugle-note had also sounded—the same which the soldiers had learned to dread. 'Twas the rallying note of the greenwood men. Cloth-yard shafts began to hurtle through the air, and Robin and his men cast aside their cloaks and sprang forward, crying:

"Lockesley! Lockesley! A rescue! A rescue!"

On the instant, a terrible scene of hand-to-hand fighting followed. The Sheriff's men, though once more taken by surprise, were determined to sell this rescue dearly. They packed in closely and stubbornly about the condemned man and Much and the palmer, and it was only by desperate rushes that the foresters made an opening in the square. Ugly cuts and bruises were exchanged freely; and lucky was the man who escaped with only these. Many of the onlookers, who had long hated the Sheriff and felt sympathy for Robin's men, also plunged into the conflict—although they could not well keep out of it, in sooth! —and aided the rescuers no little.

At last with a mighty onrush, Robin cleaved a way through the press to the scaffold itself, and not a second too soon; for two men with pikes had leaped upon the cart, and were in the act of thrusting down upon the palmer and Will Stutely. A mighty upward blow from Robin's good blade sent the pike flying from the hand of one, while a well-directed arrow from the outskirts pierced the other fellow's throat.

"God save you, master!" cried Will Stutely joyfully. "I had begun to fear that I would never see your face again."

"A rescue!" shouted the outlaws afresh, and the soldiery became faint-hearted and 'gan to give back. But the field was not yet won, for they retreated in close order toward the East gate, resolved to hem the attackers within the city walls. Here again, however, they were in error, since the outlaws did not go out by their nearest gate. They made a sally in that direction, in order to mislead the soldiery, then abruptly turned and headed for the West gate, which was still guarded by Arthur-a-Bland.

The Sheriff's men raised an exultant shout at this, thinking they had the enemy trapped. Down they charged after them, but the outlaws made good their lead, and soon got through the gate and over the bridge which had been let down by Arthur-a-Bland.

Close upon their heels came the soldiers—so close, that Arthur had no time to close the gate again or raise the bridge. So he threw away his key and fell in with the yeomen, who now began their retreat up the long hill to the woods.

On this side the town, the road leading to the forest was long and almost unprotected. The greenwood men were therefore in some distress, for the archers shot at them from loop-holes in the walls, and the pike-men were reinforced by a company of mounted men from the castle. But the outlaws retreated stubbornly and now and again turned to hold their pursuers at bay by a volley of arrows. Stutely was in their midst, fighting with the energy of two; and the little palmer was there also, but took no part save to keep close to Robin's side and mutter silent words as though in prayer.

Robin put his horn to his lips to sound a rally, when a flying arrow from the enemy pierced his hand. The palmer gave a little cry and sprang forward. The Sheriff, who had followed close with his men on horseback, also saw the wound and gave a great huzza.

"Ha! you will shoot no more bows for a season, master outlaw!" he shouted.

"You lie!" retorted Robin fiercely, wrenching the shaft

from his hand despite the streaming blood; "I have saved one shot for you all this day. Here, take it!"

And he fitted the same arrow, which had wounded him, upon the string of his bow and let it fly toward the Sheriff's head. The Sheriff fell forward upon his horse in mortal terror, but not so quickly as to escape unhurt. The sharp point laid bare a deep gash upon his scalp and must certainly have killed him if it had come closer.

The fall of the Sheriff discomfited his followers for the moment, and Robin's men took this chance to speed on up the hill. The palmer had whipped out a small white handkerchief and tried to staunch Robin's wound as they went. At the sight of the palmer's hand, Robin turned with a start, and pushed back the other's hood.

"Marian!" he exclaimed, "you here!"

It was indeed Maid Marian, who had helped save Will, and been in stress of battle from the first. Now she hung her head as though caught in wrong.

"I had to come, Robin," she said simply, "and I knew you would not let me come, else."

Their further talk was interrupted by an exclamation from Will Scarlet.

"By the saints, we are trapped!" he said, and pointed to the top of the hill, toward which they were pressing.

There from out a gray castle poured a troop of men, armed with pikes and axes, who shouted and came running down upon them. At the same instant, the Sheriff's men also renewed their pursuit.

"Alas!" cried poor Marian, "we are undone! There is no way of escape!"

"Courage, dear heart!" said Robin, drawing her close to him. But his own spirit sank as he looked about for some outlet.

Then—oh, joyful sight!— he recognized among the foremost of those coming from the castle the once doleful knight, Sir Richard of the Lea. He was smiling now, and greatly excited.

"A Hood! a Hood!" he cried; "a rescue!"

Never were there more welcome sights and sounds than these. With a great cheer the outlaws raced up the hill to meet their new friends; and soon the whole force had gained the shelter of the castle. Bang! went the bridge as it swung back up, with great clanking of chains. Clash! went one great door upon the other, as they shut in the outlaw band, and shut out the Sheriff, who dashed up at the head of his men, his face streaked with blood and inflamed with rage.

XXI

how Sir Richard of the Lea Repaid His Debt

The proud Sheriff loud 'gan cry
  And said, "Thou traitor knight,
Thou keepest here the King's enemy
  Against the laws and right."

OPEN the gates!" shouted the Sheriff hoarsely, to the sentinel upon the walls. "Open, I say, in the King's name!"

"Why, who are you to come thus brawling upon my premises?" asked a haughty voice; and Sir Richard himself stepped forth upon the turret.

"You know me well, traitor knight!" said the Sheriff, "now give up into my hands the enemy of the King whom you have sheltered against the laws and right."

"Fair and softly, sir," quoth the knight smoothly. "I well avow that I have done certain deeds this day. But I have done them upon mine own land, which you now trespass upon; and I shall answer only to the King—whom God preserve!—for my actions."

"Thou soft-spoken villain!" said the Sheriff, still in a towering passion. "I, also, serve the King; and if these outlaws are not given up to me at once, I shall lay siege to the castle and burn it with fire."

"First show me your warrants," said Sir Richard curtly.

"My word is enough! Am I not Sheriff of Nottingham?"

"If you are, in sooth," retorted the knight, "you should know that you have no authority within my lands unless you bear the King's order. In the meantime, go mend your manners, lording."

And Sir Richard snapped his fingers and disappeared from the walls. The Sheriff, after lingering a few moments longer in hope of further parley, was forced to withdraw, swearing fiercely.

"The King's order!" muttered he. "That shall I have without delay, as well as this upstart knight's estates; for King Richard is lately returned, I hear, from the Holy Land."

Meanwhile the knight had gone back to Robin Hood and the two men greeted each other right gladly.

"Well met, bold Robin!" cried he, taking him in his arms. "Well met, indeed! The Lord has lately prospered me, and I was minded this day to ride forth and repay my debt to you."

"And so you have," answered Robin gayly.

"Nay, 'twas nothing—this small service!" said the knight. "I meant the moneys coming to you."

"They have all been repaid," said Robin; "my lord of Hereford himself gave them to me."

"The exact sum?" asked the knight.

"The exact sum," answered Robin, winking solemnly.

Sir Richard smiled, but said no more at the time. Robin was made to rest until dinner should be served. Meanwhile a leech bound up his hand with ointment, promising him that he should soon have its use again. Some half-score others of the yeomen had been hurt in the fight, but luckily none of grave moment. They were all bandaged and made happy by bumpers of ale.

At dinner Sir Richard presented Robin to his wife and

son. The lady was stately and gracious, and made much of Marian, whom she had known as a little girl and who was now clothed more seemly for a dinner than in monkish garments. The young esquire was a goodly youth and bade fair to make as stout a knight as his father.

The feast was a joyous event. There were two long tables, and two hundred men sat down at them, and ate and drank and afterward sang songs. An hundred and forty of these men wore Lincoln green and called Robin Hood their chief. Never, I ween, had there been a more gallant company at table in Lea Castle!

That night the foresters tarried within the friendly walls, and the next day took leave; though Sir Richard protested that they should have made a longer stay. And he took Robin aside to his strong room and pressed him again to take the four hundred golden pounds. But his guest was firm.

"Keep the money, for it is your own," said Robin; "I have but made the Bishop return that which he extorted unjustly."

Sir Richard thanked him in a few earnest words, and asked him and all his men to visit the armory, before they departed. And therein they saw, placed apart, an hundred and forty stout yew bows of cunning make, with fine waxen silk strings; and an hundred and forty sheaves of arrows. Every shaft was a just ell long, set with peacock's feathers, and notched with silver. And Sir Richard's fair lady came forward and with her own hands gave each yeoman a bow and a sheaf.

"In sooth, these are poor presents we have made you, good Robin Hood," said Sir Richard; "but they carry with them a thousand times their weight in gratitude."

The Sheriff made good his threat to inform the King. Forth rode he to London town upon the week following, his scalp wound having healed sufficiently to permit him to travel. This time he did not seek out Prince John, but asked audience with King Richard of the Lion Heart himself. His Majesty had but lately returned from the crusades, and was just then looking into the state of his kingdom. So the Sheriff found ready audience.

Then to him the Sheriff spoke at length concerning Robin Hood; how that for many months the outlaws had defied the King, and slain the King's deer; how Robin had gathered about him the best archers in all the countryside; and, finally, how the traitorous knight Sir Richard of the Lea had rescued the band when capture seemed certain, and refused to deliver them up to justice.

The King heard him through with attention, and quoth he:

"Meseems I have heard of this same Robin Hood, and his men, and also seen somewhat of their prowess. Did not these same outlaws shoot in a royal tourney at Finsbury Field?"

"They did, Your Majesty, under a royal amnesty."

In this speech the Sheriff erred, for the King asked quickly:

"How came they last to the Fair at Nottingham—by stealth?"

"Yes, Your Majesty."

"Did you forbid them to come?"

"No, Your Majesty. That is——"

"Speak out!"

"For the good of the shire," began the Sheriff again, falteringly, "we did proclaim an amnesty; but 'twas because these men had proved a menace——"

"Now by my halidom!" quoth the King, while his brow grew black. "Such treachery would be unknown in the camp of the Saracen; and yet we call ourselves a Christian people!"

The Sheriff kept silence through very fear and shame; then the King began speech again:

"Nathless, my lord Sheriff, we promise to look into this matter. Those outlaws must be taught that there is but one King in England, and that he stands for the law."

So the Sheriff was dismissed, with very mixed feelings, and went his way home to Nottingham town.

A fortnight later the King began to make good his word, by riding with a small party of knights to Lea Castle. Sir Richard was advised of the cavalcade's approach, and quickly recognized his royal master in the tall knight who rode in advance. Hasting to open wide his castle gates he went forth to meet the King and fell on one knee and kissed his stirrup. For Sir Richard, also, had been with the King to the Holy Land, and they had gone on many adventurous quests together.

The King bade him rise, and dismounted from his own horse to greet him as a brother-in-arms; and arm-in-arm they went into the castle, while bugles and trumpets sounded forth joyous welcome in honor of the great occasion.

After the King had rested and supped, he turned upon the knight and with grave face inquired:

"What is this I hear about your castle's becoming a nest and harbor for outlaws?"

Then Sir Richard of the Lea, divining that the Sheriff had been at the King's ear with his story, made a clean breast of all he knew: how that the outlaws had befriended him in sore need—as they had befriended others—and how that he had given them only knightly protection in return.

The King liked the story well, for his own soul was one of chivalry. And he asked other questions about Robin Hood, and heard of the ancient wrong done his father before him, and of Robin's own enemies, and of his manner of living.

"In sooth," cried King Richard, springing up, "I must see this bold fellow for myself! An you will entertain my little company, and be ready to sally forth, upon the second day, in quest of me if need were, I shall e'en fare alone into the greenwood to seek an adventure with him."

But of this adventure you shall be told in the next tale; for I have already shown you how Sir Richard of the Lea repaid his debt, with interest.

XXII

how King Richard Came to Sherwood Forest

King Richard hearing of the pranks
Of Robin Hood and his men,
He much admired and more desired
To see both him and them.

* *

Then Robin takes a can of ale:
"Come let us now begin;
And every man shall have his can;
Here's a health unto the King!"

FRIAR TUCK had nursed Little John's wounded knee so skilfully that it was now healed. In sooth, the last part of the nursing depended more upon strength than skill; for it consisted chiefly of holding down the patient, by main force, to his cot. Little John had felt so well that he had insisted upon getting up before the wound was healed; and he would have done so, if the friar had not piled some holy books upon his legs and sat upon his stomach. Under this vigorous treatment Little John was constrained to lie quiet until the friar gave him leave to get up. At last he had this leave, and he and the friar went forth to join the rest of the band, who were right glad to see them, you may be sure. They sat around a big fire, for 'twas a chilly evening, and feasted and made merry, in great content.

A cold rain set in, later, but the friar wended his way back, nathless, to his little hermitage. There he made himself a cheerful blaze, and changed his dripping robe, and had sat himself down, with a sigh of satisfaction, before a tankard of hot mulled wine and a pasty, when suddenly a voice was heard on the outside, demanding admission. His kennel of dogs set up furious uproar, on the instant, by way of proving the fact of a stranger's presence.

"Now by Saint Peter!" growled the friar, "who comes here at this unseemly hour? Does he take this for a hostelry? Move on, friend, else my mulled wine will get cold!"

So saying he put the tankard to his lips, when a thundering rap sounded upon the door-panel, making it to quiver, and causing Tuck almost to drop his tankard; while an angry voice shouted:

"Ho! Within there! Open, I say!"

"Go your way in peace!" roared back the friar; "I can do nothing for you. 'Tis but a few miles to Gamewell, if you know the road."

"But I do not know the road, and if I did I would not budge another foot. 'Tis wet without and dry within. So, open, without further parley!"

"A murrain seize you for disturbing a holy man in his prayers!" muttered Tuck savagely. Nathless, he was fain to unbar the door in order to keep it from being battered down. Then lighting a torch at his fire and whistling for one of his dogs, he strode forth to see who his visitor might be.

The figure of a tall knight clad in a black coat of mail, with plumed helmet, stood before him. By his side stood his horse, also caparisoned in rich armor.

"Have you no supper, brother?" asked the Black Knight curtly. "I must beg of you a bed and a bit of roof, for this night, and fain would refresh my body ere I sleep."

"I have no room that even your steed would deign to accept, Sir Knight; and naught save a crust of bread and pitcher of water."

"I' faith, I can smell better fare than that, brother, and must e'en force my company upon you, though I shall recompense it for gold in the name of the church. As for my horse, let him but be blanketed and put on the sheltered side of the house."

And without further parley the knight boldly strode past Tuck and his dog and entered the hermitage. Something about his masterful air pleased Tuck, in spite of his churlishness.

"Sit you down, Sir Knight," quoth he, "and I will fasten up your steed, and find him somewhat in the shape of grain. Half, also, of my bed and board is yours, this night; but we shall see later who is the better man, and is to give the orders!"

"With all my soul!" said the knight, laughing. "I can pay my keeping in blows or gold as you prefer."

The friar presently returned and drew up a small table near the fire.

"Now, Sir Knight," quoth he, "put off your sword and helm and such other war-gear as it pleases you, and help me lay this table, for I am passing hungry."

The knight did as he was told, and put aside the visor which had hid his face. He was a bronzed and bearded man with blue eyes, and hair shot with gold, haughty but handsome withal.

Then once again the priest sat him down to his pasty and mulled wine, right hopefully. He spoke his grace with some haste, and was surprised to hear his guest respond fittingly in the Latin tongue. Then they attacked the wine and pasty valiantly, and the Black Knight made good his word of being in need of refreshment. Tuck looked ruefully at the rapidly disappearing food, but came to grudge it not, by reason of the stories with which his guest enlivened the meal. The wine and warmth of the room had cheered them both, and they were soon laughing uproariously as the best of comrades in the world. The Black Knight, it seemed, had traveled everywhere. He had been on crusades, had fought the courteous Saladin, had been in prison, and often in peril. But now he spoke of it lightly, and laughed it off, and made himself so friendly that Friar Tuck was like to choke with merriment.

"One more bumper before we turn in," said the now mellow friar. He raised a horn of wine and held it high. "To the health of the King, and confusion to his enemies!"

"A right good toast," quoth the other, extending his cup.

So passed the time till late; and the two fell asleep together, one on each side of the table which they had cleared of the platters.

In the morning Friar Tuck awoke disposed again to be surly, but was speedily mollified by the sight of the Black Knight who had already risen gay as a lark, washed his face and hands, and was now stirring a hot gruel over the fire.

"By my faith, I make a sorry host!" cried Tuck, springing to his feet. And later as they sat at breakfast, he added, "I want not your gold, of which you spoke last night; but instead I will do what I can to speed you on your way whenever you wish to depart."

"Then tell me," said the knight, "how I may find Robin Hood the outlaw; for I have a message to him from the King. All day yesterday I sought him, but found him not."

Friar Tuck lifted up his hands in holy horror. "I am a lover of peace, Sir Knight, and do not consort with Robin's bold fellows."

"Nay, I think no harm of Master Hood," said the knight; "but much I yearn to have speech with him in mine own person."

"If that be all, mayhap I can guide you to his haunts," said Tuck, who foresaw in this knight a possible gold-bag for Robin. "In sooth, I could not well live in these woods without hearing somewhat of the outlaws; but matters of religion are my chief joy and occupation."

"I will go with you, brother," said the Black Knight.

So without more ado they went their way into the forest, the knight riding upon his charger, and Tuck pacing along demurely by his side on a mule.

The day had dawned clear and bright, and now with the sun a good three hours high a sweet autumn fragrance was in the air. The wind had just that touch of coolness in it which sets the hunter's blood to tingling; and every creature of nature seemed bounding with joyous life.

The knight sniffed the fresh air in delight.

"By my halidom!" quoth he; "but the good greenwood is the best place to live in, after all! What court or capital can equal this, for full-blooded men?"

"None of this earth," replied Tuck smilingly. And once more his heart warmed toward this courteous stranger.

They had not proceeded more than three or four miles along the way from Fountain Abbey to Barnesdale, when of a sudden the bushes just ahead of them parted and a well-knit man with curling brown hair stepped into the road and laid his hand upon the knight's bridle.

It was Robin Hood. He had seen Friar Tuck, a little way back, and shrewdly suspected his plan. Tuck, however, feigned not to know him at all.

"Hold!" cried Robin; "I am in charge of the highway this day, and must exact an accounting from all passers-by."

"Who is it bids me hold?" asked the knight quietly. "I am not i' the habit of yielding to one man."

"Then here are others to keep me company," said Robin clapping his hands. And instantly a half-score other stalwart fellows came out of the bushes and stood beside him.

"We be yeomen of the forest, Sir Knight," continued Robin, "and live under the greenwood tree. We have no means of support—thanks to the tyranny of our over-lords —other than the aid which fat churchmen, and goodly knights like yourselves can give. And as ye have churches and rents, both, and gold in great plenty, we beseech ye for Saint Charity to give us some of your spending.

"I am but a poor monk, good sir!" said Friar Tuck in a whining voice, "and am on my way to the shrine of Saint Dunstan, if your worshipfulness will permit."

"Tarry a space with us," answered Robin, biting back a smile, "and we will speed you on your way."

The Black Knight now spoke again. "But we are messengers of the King," quoth he; "His Majesty himself tarries near here and would have speech with Robin Hood."

"God save the King!" said Robin doffing his cap loyally; "and all that wish him well! I am Robin Hood, but I say cursed be the man who denies our liege King's sovereignty!"

"Have a care!" said the knight, "or you shall curse yourself!"

"Nay, not so," replied Robin curtly; "the King has no more devoted subject than I. Nor have I despoiled aught of his save, mayhap, a few deer for my hunger. My chief war is against the clergy and barons of the land who bear down upon the poor. But I am glad," he continued, "that I have met you here; and before we end you shall be my friend and taste of our greenwood cheer."

"But what is the reckoning?" asked the knight. "For I am told that some of your feasts are costly."

"Nay," responded Robin, waving his hands, "you are from the King. Nathless—how much money is in your purse?"

"I have no more than forty gold pieces, seeing that I have lain a fortnight at Nottingham with the King, and have spent some goodly amounts upon other lordings," replied the knight.

Robin took the forty pounds and gravely counted it. One-half he gave to his men and bade them drink the King's health with it. The other half he handed back to the knight.

"Sir," said he courteously, "have this for your spending. If you lie with kings and lordings overmuch, you are like to need it."

"Gramercy!" replied the other smiling. "And now lead on to your greenwood hostelry."

So Robin went on one side of the knight's steed, and Friar Tuck on the other, and the men went before and behind till they came to the open glade before the caves of Barnesdale. Then Robin drew forth his bugle and winded the three signal blasts of the band. Soon there came a company of yeomen with its leader, and another, and a third, and a fourth, till there were sevenscore yeomen in sight. All were dressed in new livery of Lincoln green, and carried new bows in their hands and bright short swords at their belts. And every man bent his knee to Robin Hood ere taking his place before the board, which was already set.

At Robin's request, the knight laid aside his suit of heavy armor, and was given a loose cloak, the better to enjoy the feast. With his helmet removed and the sunlight striking his ruddy hair he made a goodly picture.

A handsome dark-haired page stood at Robin's right hand to pour his wine and that of the knightly guest; while the knight marveled much at all he saw, and said within himself:

"These men of Robin Hood's give him more obedience than my fellows give to me."

At the signal from Robin the dinner began. There was venison and fowl and fish and wheaten cake and ale and red wine in great plenty, and 'twas a goodly sight to see the smiles upon the hungry yeomen's faces.

First they listened to an unctuous grace from Friar Tuck, and then Robin lifted high a tankard of ale.

"Come, let us now begin," quoth he, "and every man shall have his can. In honor of our guest who comes with royal word, here's a health unto the King!"

The guest responded heartily to this toast, and round

about the board it went, the men cheering noisily for King Richard!

After the feast was over, Robin turned to his guest and said, "Now you shall see what life we lead, so that you may report faithfully, for good or bad, unto the King."

So at a signal from him, the men rose up and smartly bent their bows for practice, while the knight was greatly astonished at the smallness of their targets. A wand was set up, far down the glade, and thereon was balanced a garland of roses. Whosoever failed to speed his shaft through the garland, without knocking it off the wand, was to submit to a buffet from the hand of Friar Tuck.

"Ho, ho!" cried the knight, as his late traveling companion rose up and bared his brawny arm ready for service; "so you, my friend, are Friar Tuck!"

"I have not gainsaid it," replied Tuck, growling at having betrayed himself. "But chastisement is a rule of the church, and I am seeking the good of these stray sheep."

The knight said no more, though his eyes twinkled; and the shooting began.

David of Doncaster shot first and landed safely through the rose garland. Then came Allan-a-Dale and Little John and Stutely and Scarlet and many of the rest, while the knight held his breath from very amazement. Each fellow shot truly through the garland, until Middle the tinker—not to be outdone—stepped up for a trial. But alas! while he made a fair shot for a townsman, the arrow never came within a handbreadth of the outer rim of the garland.

"Come hither, fellow," said Little John coaxingly. "The priest would bless thee with his open hand."

Then because Middle made a wry face, as though he had already received the buffet, and loitered in his steps,

Arthur-a-Bland and Will Stutely seized him by the arms and stood him before the friar. Tuck's big arm flashed through the air—"whoof!" and stopped suddenly against the tinker's ear; while Middle himself went rolling over and over on the grass. He was stopped by a small bush, and up he sat, thrusting his head through it, rubbing his ear and blinking up at the sky as though the stars had fallen and struck him. The yeomen roared with merriment, and as for the knight he laughed till the tears came out of his blue eyes and rolled down his face.

After Middle's mishap, others of the band seemed to lose their balance, and fared in the same fashion. The garland would topple over in a most impish way at every breath, although the arrows went through it. So Middle 'gan to feel better when he saw this one and that one tumbling on the sward.

At last came Robin's turn. He shot carefully, but as bad luck would have it the shaft was ill feathered and swerved sidewise so that it missed the garland by full three fingers. Then a great roar went up from the whole company; for 'twas rare that they saw their leader miss his mark. Robin flung his bow upon the ground from very vexation.

"A murrain take it!" quoth he. "The arrow was sadly winged. I felt the poor feather upon it as it left my fingers!"

Then suddenly seizing his bow again, he sped three shafts as fast as he could send them, and every one went clean through the garland.

"By Saint George!" muttered the knight. "Never before saw I such shooting in all Christendom!"

The band cheered heartily at these last shots; but Will Scarlet came up gravely to Robin.

"Pretty shooting, master!" quoth he, "but 'twill not save you from paying for the bad arrow. So walk up and take your medicine!"

"Nay, that may not be!" protested Robin. "The good friar belongs to my company and has no authority to lift hands against me. But you, Sir Knight, stand as it were for the King. I pray you, serve out my blow."

"Not so!" said Friar Tuck. "My son, you forget I stand for the church, which is greater even than the King."

"Not in merry England," said the knight in a deep voice.

Then rising to his feet, he added, "I stand ready to serve you, Master Hood."

"Now out upon ye for an upstart knight!" cried Friar Tuck. "I told you last night, sirrah, that we should yet see who was the better man! So we will e'en prove it now, and thus settle who is to pay Robin Hood."

"Good!" said Robin, "for I want not to start a dispute between church and state."

"Good!" also said the knight. " 'Tis an easy way to end prattling. Come, friar, strike and ye dare. I will give you first blow."

"You prate full bravely," said the friar; "but have at ye! Down you shall go, if you were Goliath of Gath."

Once more the priest's brawny arm flashed through the air, and struck with a "whoof!" But to the amazement of all, the knight did not budge from his tracks, though the upper half of his body swerved slightly to ease the force of the blow. A loud shout burst from the yeomen at this, for the friar's fist was proverbial, and few of those present had not felt the force of it in times past.

"Now 'tis my turn," said his antagonist coolly, casting aside his gauntlet. And with one blow of his fist the knight sent the friar spinning to the ground.

If there had been uproar and shouting before, it was as naught to the noise which now broke forth. Every fellow held his sides or rolled upon the ground from laughter; every fellow, save one, and that was Robin Hood.

"Out of the frying-pan into the fire!" thought he. "I wish I had let the friar box my ears, after all!"

Robin's plight did, indeed, seem a sorry one, before the steel muscles of this stranger. But he was saved from a tumble heels over head by an unlooked-for diversion. A horn winded in the glade, and a party of knights were seen approaching.

"To your arms!" cried Robin, hurriedly seizing his sword and bow.

" 'Tis Sir Richard of the Lea!" cried another, as the troop came nearer.

And so it was. Sir Richard spurred forward his horse and dashed up to the camp while the outlaws stood at stiff attention. When he had come near the spot where the Black Knight stood—though now bareheaded and looking more monk than knight—he dismounted and knelt before him.

"I trust Your Majesty has not needed our arms before," he said humbly.

"It is the King!" cried Will Scarlet, falling upon his knees.

"The King!" echoed Robin Hood after a moment of dumb wonderment; and he and all his men bent reverently upon their knees, as one man.

XXIII

how Robin Hood and Maid Marian Were Wed

"Stand up again," then said the King,
  "I'll thee thy pardon give;
Stand up, my friend; who can
    contend,
  When I give leave to live?"

* *

Then Robin Hood began a health
  To Marian, his only dear;
And his yeomen all, both comely **and**
    tall,
  Did quickly bring up the rear.

"Your pardon, sire!" exclaimed
Robin Hood. "Pardon, from your royal bounty, for these
my men who stand ready to serve you all your days!"

Richard of the Lion Heart looked grimly about over
the kneeling band.

"Is it as your leader says?" he asked.

"Aye, my lord King!" burst from sevenscore throats at
once.

"We be not outlaws from choice alone," continued
Robin; "but have been driven to outlawry through oppres-

272

sion. Grant us grace and royal protection, and we will forsake the greenwood and follow the King."

Richard's eyes sparkled as he looked from one to another of this stalwart band, and he thought within himself that here, indeed, was a royal body-guard worth the while.

"Swear!" he said in his full rich voice; "swear that you, Robin Hood, and all your men from this day henceforth will serve the King!"

"We swear!" came once more the answering shout from the yeomen.

"Arise, then," said King Richard. "I give you all free pardon, and will speedily put your service to the test. For I love such archers as you have shown yourselves to be, and it were a sad pity to decree such men to death. England could not produce the like again, for many a day. But, in sooth, I cannot allow you to roam in the forest and shoot my deer; nor to take the law of the land into your own hands. Therefore, I now appoint you to be Royal Archers and mine own especial body-guard. There be one or two civil matters to settle with certain Norman noblemen, in which I crave your aid. Thereafter, the half of your number, as may later be determined, shall come back to these woodlands as Royal Foresters. Mayhap you will show as much zeal in protecting my preserves as you have formerly shown in hunting them. Where, now, is that outlaw known as Little John? Stand forth!"

"Here, sire," quoth the giant, doffing his cap.

"Good master Little John," said the King, looking him over approvingly. "Could your weak sinews stand the strain of an office in the shire? If so, you are this day Sheriff of Nottingham; and I trust you will make a better official than the man you relieve."

"I shall do my best, sire," said Little John, great astonishment and gladness in his heart.

"Master Scarlet, stand forth," said the King; and then addressing him: "I have heard somewhat of your tale," quoth he, "and that your father was the friend of my father. Now, therefore, accept the royal pardon and resume the care of your family estates; for your father must be growing old. And come you to London next Court day and we shall see if there be a knighthood vacant."

Likewise the King called for Will Stutely and made him Chief of the Royal Archers. Then he summoned Friar Tuck to draw near.

"I crave my King's pardon," said the priest, humbly enough; "for who am I to lift my hand against the Lord's anointed?"

"Nay, the Lord sent the smiter to thee without delay," returned Richard smiling; "and 'tis not for me to continue a quarrel between church and state. So what can I do for you in payment of last night's hospitality? Can I find some fat living where there are no wicked to chastise, and where the work is easy and comfortable?"

"Not so, my lord," replied Tuck. "I wish only for peace in this life. Mine is a simple nature and I care not for the fripperies and follies of court life. Give me a good meal and a cup of right brew, health, and enough for the day, and I ask no more."

Richard sighed. "You ask the greatest thing in the world, brother—contentment. It is not mine to give or to deny. But ask your God for it, and if belike he grant it, then ask it also in behalf of your King." He glanced around once more at the foresters. "Which one of you is Allan-a-Dale?" he asked; and when Allan had come forward, "So," said the King with sober face, "you are that errant minstrel who stole a bride at Plympton, despite her would-be groom and attending Bishop. I heard something of this in former days. Now what excuse have you to make?"

"Only that I loved her, sire, and she loved me," said Allan, simply; "and the Norman lord would have married her perforce, because of her lands."

"Which have since been forfeited by the Bishop of Hereford," added Richard. "But my lord Bishop must disgorge them; and from to-morrow you and Mistress Dale are to return to them and live in peace and loyalty. And if ever I need your harp at Court, stand ready to attend me, and bring also the lady. Speaking of ladies," he continued, turning to Robin Hood, who had stood silent, wondering if a special punishment were being reserved for him, "did you not have a sweetheart who was once at Court—one Mistress Marian? What has become of her, that you should have forgotten her?"

"Nay, Your Majesty," said the black-eyed page coming forward blushingly; "Robin has not forgotten me!"

"So!" said the King, bending to kiss her small hand in all gallantry. "Verily, as I have already thought within myself, this Master Hood is better served than the King in his palace! But are you not the only child of the late Earl of Huntingdon?"

"I am, sire, though there be some who say that Robin Hood's father was formerly the rightful Earl of Huntingdon. Nathless, neither he is advantaged nor I, for the estates are confiscate."

"Then they shall be restored forthwith!" cried the King; "and lest you two should revive the ancient quarrel over them, I bestow them upon you jointly. Come forward, Robin Hood."

Robin came and knelt before his King. Richard drew

his sword and touched him upon the shoulder.

"Rise, Robin Fitzooth, Earl of Huntingdon!" he exclaimed, while a mighty cheer arose from the band and rent the air of the forest. "The first command I give you, my lord Earl," continued the King when quiet was restored, "is to marry Mistress Marian without delay."

"May I obey all Your Majesty's commands as willingly!" cried the new Earl of Huntingdon, drawing the old earl's daughter close to him. "The ceremony shall take place to-morrow, an this maid is willing."

"She makes little protest," said the King; "so I shall e'en give away the bride myself!"

Then the King chatted with others of the foresters, and made himself as one of them for the evening, rejoicing that he could have this careless freedom of the woods. And Much, the miller's son, and Arthur-a-Bland, and Middle, and Stutely and Scarlet and Little John and others played at the quarter-staff, giving and getting many lusty blows. Then as the shades of night drew on, the whole company — knights and foresters — supped and drank around a blazing fire, while Allan sang sweetly to the thrumming of the harp, and the others joined in the chorus.

'Twas a happy, care-free night—this last one together under the greenwood tree. Robin could not help feeling an undertone of sadness that it was to be the last; for the charm of the woodland was still upon him. But he knew 'twas better so, and that the new life with Marian and in the service of his King would bring its own joys.

Then the night deepened, the fire sank, but was replenished and the company lay down to rest. The King, at his own request, spent the night in the open. Thus they slept —King and subject alike—out under the stars, cared for lovingly by Nature, kind mother of us all.

In the morning the company was early astir and on their way to Nottingham. It was a goodly cavalcade. First rode King Richard of the Lion Heart, with his tall figure set forth by the black armor and waving plume in his helm. Then came Sir Richard of the Lea with fourscore knights and men-at-arms. And after them came Robin Hood and Maid Marian riding upon milk-white steeds. Allan-a-Dale also escorted Mistress Dale on horseback, for she was to be matron-of-honor at the wedding. These were followed by sevenscore archers clad in their bravest Lincoln green, and with their new bows unstrung in token of peace.

Outside the gates of Nottingham town they were halted.

"Who comes here?" asked the warder's surly voice.

"Open to the King of England!" came back the clear answer, and the gates were opened and the bridge let down without delay.

Almost before the company had crossed the moat the news spread through the town like wildfire.

"The King is here! The King is here, and hath taken Robin Hood!"

From every corner flocked the people to see the company pass; and wildly did they cheer for the King, who rode smilingly with bared head down through the market-place.

At the far end of it, he was met by the Sheriff who came up puffing in his haste to do the King honor. He fairly turned green with rage when he saw Sir Richard of the Lea and Robin Hood in the royal company, but made low obeisance to his master.

"Sir Sheriff," quoth the King, "I have come to rid the shire of outlaws, according to my promise. There be none left, for all have now taken service with their King. And lest there should be further outbreak, I have determined to place in charge of this shire a man who fears no other man in it. Master Little John is hereby created Sheriff of Nottingham, and you will turn over the keys to him forth-with."

The Sheriff bowed, but dared utter no word. Then the King turned to the Bishop of Hereford, who had also come up to pay his respects.

"Harkee, my lord Bishop," quoth he, "the stench of your evil actions has reached our nostrils. We shall demand strict accounting for certain seizures of lands and certain acts of oppression which ill become a churchman. But of this, later. This afternoon you must officiate at the wedding of two of our company, in Nottingham Church. So make you ready."

The Bishop also bowed and departed, glad to escape a severer censure for the time.

The company then rode on to the Mansion House, where the King held high levee through all the noon hours, and the whole town made a holiday.

In the afternoon the way from the Mansion House to Nottingham Church was lined with cheering people, as the wedding party passed by. The famous bow-men were gazed at as curiously as though they had been wild animals, but were cheered none the less. Robin who had long been held in secret liking was now doubly popular since he had the King's favor.

Along the way ahead of the King and the smiling bride and groom-to-be ran little maids strewing flowers; while streamers floated in greeting from the windows. I ween, the only hearts that were not glad this day were those of the old Sheriff, and of his proud daughter, who peered between the shutters of her window and was like to eat out her heart from envy and hatred.

At last the party reached the church, where the King dismounted lightly from his horse and helped the bride to alight; while Will Scarlet, the best man, assisted Mistress Dale. Within the church they found the Bishop robed in state, and by his side Friar Tuck who had been especially deputed to assist.

The service was said in Latin, while the organ pealed forth softly. The King gave away the bride, as he had said, and afterwards claimed first kiss for his pains. Then the happy party dispersed, and Robin and Marian passed out again through the portal, man and wife.

Out through the cheering streets they fared, while the greenwood men ran ahead and flung gold pennies right and left in their joy, and bade the people drink the health of the young couple and the King. Then the whole party took horse at Will Scarlet's earnest wish, and went down to Gamewell Lodge, where the old Squire George wept for joy at seeing his son and the King and the wedding-party. That night they spent there, and feasted, and the next day Sir Richard of the Lea claimed them.

And thus, amid rejoicing and kingly favor, Robin Hood, the new Earl of Huntingdon, and his bride began their wedded life.

XXIV

how Robin Hood Met His Death

"Give me my bent bow in my hand,
  And a broad arrow I'll let flee;
And where this arrow is taken up,
  There shall my grave digg'd be."

Now by good rights this story should end with the wedding of Robin Hood and Maid Marian; for do not many pleasant tales end with a wedding and the saying, "and they lived happy ever after"? But this is a true account—in so far as we can find the quaint old ballads which tell of it—and so we must follow one more of these songs and learn how Robin, after living many years longer, at last came to seek his grave. And the story of it runs in this wise.

Robin Hood and his men, now the Royal Archers, went with King Richard of the Lion Heart through England settling certain private disputes which had arisen among the Norman barons while the King was gone to the Holy Land. Then the King proceeded amid great pomp and rejoicing to the palace at London, and Robin, the new Earl of Huntingdon, brought his Countess thither where she became one of the finest ladies of the Court.

The Royal Archers were now divided into two bands, and one-half of them were retained in London, while the

281

other half returned to Sherwood and Barnesdale, there to guard the King's preserves.

Several months passed by, and Robin began to chafe under the restraint of city life. He longed for the fresh pure air of the greenwood, and the rollicking society of his yeomen. One day, upon seeing some lads at archery practice upon a green he could not help but lament, saying, "Woe is me! I fear my hand is fast losing its old-time cunning at the bow-string!"

Finally he became so distraught that he asked leave to travel in foreign lands, and this was granted him. He took Maid Marian with him, and together they went through many strange countries. Finally in an Eastern land a great grief came upon Robin. Marian sickened of a plague and died. They had been married but five years, and Robin felt as though all the light had gone out of his life.

He wandered about the world for a few months longer, trying to forget his grief, then came back to the Court, at London, and sought some commission in active service. But, unluckily, Richard was gone again upon his adventures, and Prince John, who acted as Regent, had never been fond of Robin. He received him with a sarcastic smile.

"Go forth into the greenwood," said he coldly, "and kill some more of the King's deer. Belike, then, the King will make you a Prime Minister, at the very least, upon his return."

The taunt fired Robin's blood. He had been in a morose mood, ever since his dear wife's death. He answered Prince John hotly, and the Prince bade his guards seize him and cast him into the Tower.

After lying there for a few weeks, he was released by the faithful Stutely and the remnant of the Royal Archers, and all together they fled the city and made their way to the greenwood. There Robin blew the old familiar call, which all had known and loved so well. Up came running the remainder of the band, who had been Royal Foresters, and when they saw their old master they embraced his knees and kissed his hands, and fairly cried for joy that he had come again to them. And one and all foreswore fealty to Prince John, and lived quietly with Robin in the greenwood, doing harm to none and only awaiting the time when King Richard should come again.

But King Richard came not again, and would never need his Royal Guard more. Tidings presently reached them, of how he had met his death in a foreign land, and how John reigned as King in his stead. The proof of these events followed soon after, when there came striding through the glade the big, familiar form of Little John.

"Art come to arrest us?" called out Robin, as he ran forward and embraced his old comrade.

"Nay, I am not come as the Sheriff of Nottingham, thanks be," answered Little John. "The new King has deposed me, and 'tis greatly to my liking, for I have long desired to join you here again in the greenwood."

Then were the rest of the band right glad at this news, and toasted Little John royally.

The new King waged fierce war upon the outlaws, soon after this, and sent so many scouting parties into Sherwood and Barnesdale that Robin and his men left these woods for a time and went to Derbyshire, near Haddon Hall. A curious pile of stone is shown to this day as the ruins of Robin's Castle, where the bold outlaw is believed to have defied his enemies for a year or more. At any rate King John found so many troubles of his own, after a time, that he ceased troubling the outlaws.

But in one of these last sorties Robin was wounded. The cut did not seem serious, and healed over the top; but it left a lurking fever. Daily his strength ebbed away from him, until he was in sore distress.

One day as he rode along on horseback, near Kirkley Abbey, he was seized with so violent a rush of blood to the head that he reeled and came near falling from his saddle. He dismounted weakly and knocked at the gate. A woman in black peered forth.

"Who are you that knock here?" she asked.

"Open, for the love of Heaven!" he begged. "I am Robin Hood, ill of fever and in sore straits."

At the name of Robin Hood the woman unbarred the door and admitted him. Assisting his fainting frame up a flight of stairs and into a front room, she loosed his collar and bathed his face until he was revived. Then she spoke hurriedly:

"Your fever will sink, if you are bled. See, I have provided a lancet and will open your veins, while you lie quiet."

So she bled him, and he fell into a stupor which lasted nearly all that day, so that he awoke weak and exhausted from loss of blood. . . .

He called wearily for help, but there was no response. He looked longingly through the window at the green of the forest; but he was too weak to make the leap that would be needed to reach the ground.

> He then bethought him of his horn,
>   Which hung down at his knee;
> He set his horn unto his mouth,
>   And blew out weak blasts three.

Little John was out in the forest near by, or the blasts would never have been heard. At their sound he sprang to his feet.

"Woe! woe!" he cried, "I fear my master is near dead, he blows so wearily!"

So he made haste and came running up to the door of the abbey, and knocked loudly for admittance. Failing to get reply he burst in the door with frenzied blows of his mighty fist, and soon came running up to the room where Robin lay, white and faint.

"Alas, dear master!" cried Little John in great distress; "I fear you have met with treachery! If that be so, grant me one last boon, I pray."

"What is it?" asked Robin.

"Let me burn Kirkley Hall with fire."

"Nay, good comrade," answered Robin Hood gently, "I cannot grant such a boon. The dear Christ bade us forgive all our enemies. Moreover, you know I never hurt woman in all my life; nor man when in woman's company."

He closed his eyes and fell back, so that his friend thought him dying. The great tears fell from the giant's eyes and wet his master's hand. Robin slowly rallied and seized his comrade's outstretched arm.

"Lift me up, good Little John," he said brokenly, "I want to smell the air from the good greenwood once again. Give me my good yew bow—here—here—and fix a broad arrow upon the string. Out yonder—among the oaks— where this arrow shall fall—let them dig my grave."

And with one last mighty effort he sped his shaft out of the open window, straight and true, as in the days of old, till it struck the largest oak of them all and dropped in the shadow of the trees. Then he fell back upon the sobbing breast of his devoted friend.

"'Tis the last!" he murmured, "tell the brave hearts to lay me there with the green sod under my head and feet.

And—let them lay—my bent bow at my side, for it has made sweet music in mine ears."

He rested a moment, and Little John scarce knew that he was alive. But on a sudden Robin's eyes brightened, and he seemed to think himself back once more with the band in the open forest glade. He struggled to rise.

"Ha! 'tis a fine stag, Will! And Allan, thou never didst thrum the harp more sweetly. How the light blazes! And Marian!—'tis my Marian—come at last!"

So died the body of Robin Hood; but his spirit lives on through the centuries in the deathless ballads which are sung of him, and in the hearts of men who love freedom and chivalry.

They buried him where his last arrow had fallen, and they set up a stone to mark the spot. And on the stone were graven these words:

"Here underneath this little stone
Lies Robert, Earl of Huntingdon;
Never archer as he so good,
And people called him Robin Hood.
Such outlaws as he and his men
Will England never see again."

Robin Hood

illustrated by Louis Slobodkin, is one of the series of

RAINBOW CLASSICS

Edited under the supervision of May Lamberton Becker

Typesetting by Westcott and Thomson

Printing and binding by H. Wolff

Designer: Ernst Reichl